GRIEF
and Other Stories

GRIEF

and Other Stories

THEODORE DALRYMPLE

Published by New English Review Press
a subsidiary of World Encounter Institute
PO Box 158397
Nashville, Tennessee 37215
&
27 Old Gloucester Street
London, England, WC1N 3AX

Cover Art and Design by Kendra Mallock

ISBN: 978-1-943003-16-7

First Edition

NEW ENGLISH REVIEW PRESS
newenglishreview.org

CONTENTS

I

GRIEF

WHEN KIRSTY KILLED Shannon, it was an accident: she had only meant to teach her a lesson. That was why she had pulled her to the ground by her hair, called her a f…ing slut, and banged her head on the ground.

'That'll learn you a lesson,' she screamed, as Shannon's head cracked on the paving stone.

But Shannon learned nothing from the experience because she never regained consciousness. Kirsty couldn't help thinking that she died just to spite her and get her into trouble. Shannon was like that: she thought only of herself.

Well, it had certainly landed Kirsty in trouble, big time, as she said to her mother. The cops had come, arriving a bit before the ambulance (typical!), and started to ask questions straight away, nosey bastards. Kirsty told them that she had pushed Shannon, who had fallen and banged her head on the kerb: she might have given her a slap as well (she had certainly asked for one), but she couldn't remember, it all happened so fast. But it wouldn't have been a hard slap.

At first, the cops seemed to believe her. Why shouldn't they? What reason did they have for not doing so? Suspicious bastards, as well as nosey!

They made Kirsty sign a statement. It wasn't really hers at all. She told them what had happened and they put it into their own words, which they told her to sign. Kirsty told her law-yer later that she was all shook up when she signed, and hardly knew what she was saying or doing. The cops were like that, they never treated the likes of Kirsty fair. The last time she had had anything to do with them, they had accused her of threat-ening Shannon with a knife, as if she would. Anyone could have seen it was ridiculous, she never would of used it, and anyway Shannon was a liar, everyone knew that. The case was dropped a few days later when Shannon withdrew the charges.

Shannon was no angel, everyone knew that, in fact she was a right bitch. But now she was dead, everyone was making out she was a saint or something. For one thing she was fat, even though she smoked like a chimney. She was always feeding her face. She was a slut, too; she would go with anyone, and did. You had only to look at her tattoos to know that. She had the names of her boyfriends tattooed on her arms like fighter pilots used to stick the numbers of enemy aircraft shot down on the fuse-lage of their own planes. She didn't have to make an exhibition of herself like this, show off, like. After all, she wasn't exactly a picture to start with. It was difficult to see what men saw in her, apart from willingness. Kirsty had only the names of her kids tattooed on her arms.

Kirsty and Shannon had been neighbours in Broadfields Walk, whose maisonettes were reached by a covered concrete walk where boys in grey flannel hoodies hung out. Kirsty and Shannon were even friends once upon a time; they went out clubbing together when one or other of their mothers could be persuaded to look after the kids for the night. They would both get drunk and there is nothing like vomiting together to cement a friendship.

But the friendship did not last. It changed to enmity when both of them fell pregnant for the same man, Delancey Jones. Delancey, the baby-father, took crack and admitted that he was into things; but Kirsty and Shannon each thought that he would change when she had his baby for him. He soon disappeared, however, and was off the scene, as the two women described their lives.

Their mutual jealousy persisted long after neither of them wanted Delancey back: for two people can easily quarrel over what neither of them wants, and Kirsty and Shannon continued to believe that each had betrayed the other in the most despicable way possible. Very occasionally Delancey would reappear for the night, for reasons known only to himself, and a well-wishing resident of Broadfields Walk would inform the one not selected to receive him of his sojourn with the other. A screaming match between Kirsty and Shannon would follow when next they bumped into each other, and they would trade insults: f…ing slag, slut or slapper.

Their babies were born three days apart, in the same hospital ward. Kirsty was going home as Shannon arrived. Shannon, though not very mobile, ill-advisedly gave Kirsty a slap, and the nurses had to keep them apart. When Shannon had gone, Kirsty explained to the nurses what Shannon was like.

The babies were both called Jaydon, which was another cause of friction between Kirsty and Shannon.

'Can't she think of a f…ing name for herself!' said Kirsty to her mother.

'She f…ing copied me!' said Shannon to hers. 'Just to get my goat.'

From then on, the two mothers would sometimes pass each other on the street pushing their respective Jaydons in their pushchairs. Once, Shannon even rammed her Jaydon's pushchair into Kirsty's Jaydon's pushchair, as if trying to destroy it. They had had arguments about which of the pushchairs was better, more solid, more expensive.

'What do you think you're f…ing doing, you f…ing bitch!' screamed Kirsty.

'Why don't you f…ing watch where you're going, you stupid cow!' retired Shannon.

They set about each other until passers-by intervened. The two Jaydons screamed in their pushchairs.

Of course, Kirsty's and Shannon's other children, for different baby-fathers, learnt their mothers' enmity and followed suit whenever they met.

The two Jaydons, of café-au-lait complexion, grew at more or less the same pace, though perhaps Kirsty's Jaydon was a little sturdier. Taking after the baby-father, both of them were rebels: they refused to do what they were told.

'I told you to come here, you little shit!' they would scream at their Jaydons when they ran off in the supermarket, wouldn't come back or took things from the shelves. And when the Jaydons returned to the fold, as it were, they received either a smack or a bar of chocolate, depending on how things had just gone with the newest boyfriend.

A deadly rivalry grew between Kirsty and Shannon as to whose Jaydon was the better dressed and the better supplied with toys. They had to have the latest fashion in toddlers' clothes – no hand-me-downs for them. Of course, the clothes were more expensive than the mothers could afford, but they borrowed money wherever they could (Delancey was useless, of course), and they used successive credit cards to the maximum allowed. The important thing for them was that their Jaydon should have a newer outfit, and better toys, than the other.

Being of the same age, the two Jaydons started school at the same time. By then, both Kirsty and Shannon were pleased to get them off their hands for a few hours each day, for they were both overactive, running around all the time, knocking into things and breaking them, and defiant of any kind of correction. Once, when he had just turned three, Kirsty's Jaydon turned on her when she told him to stop trying to put his fingers in an electric socket and, narrowing his eyes in an imitation of adult menace, said, 'Well f… you!'

The mothers of Broadfields Walk had no choice but to send their children to the William Wilberforce Junior School in Sebastopol Road. It was about ten minutes' walk away, if you dragged the children, and it was inevitable that Kirsty and Shannon should sometimes meet on the way and at the school gate when they came to collect the two Jaydons. Mostly they just glared at each other, but at other times what they called a war broke out between them. They called each other whore, but on a few occasions they used their free hand – the other hanging on to their respective Jaydon – to aim a blow at the other or to grab and pull the other's hair. The other mothers intervened to stop them, before they called the attention to them of what they called the Social – an eventuality that all mothers round there feared, more than an epidemic. Everyone knew of kids who had been removed into care by the all-powerful Social, and no one ever reported abuse for fear of being known as a grass. Memories were long in Broadfields Walk and nothing was ever forgotten; besides, everyone enjoyed nursing her own hatred, it gave her a warm glow inside (there were few men in the road).

Not surprisingly, the two Jaydons did not get on well. Kirsty and Shannon told them that the other Jaydon was bad, scum with whom they should not associate, because their mother was a f...ing foul-mouthed bitch. On no account, then, should Jaydon play with Jaydon, because they would catch something from one another, namely bad behaviour. Before long, the teachers had to devote a lot of time and attention to keeping the two Jaydons apart. They were in the same class – again, there was no choice in the matter – and they were put in opposite corners of the classroom, but as soon as the teacher's and the teaching assistant's back was turned, they rushed at each other, and had to be torn apart as if they were made of Velcro. Their fists were as yet too small to inflict much damage, but they could scratch one another and overturn tables and paint pots and the like. The teacher of the class had to devote at least half her time to keeping the peace between them, to the neglect of the other children, many of who had problems of their own. Playtime was the worst, of course, for then the children were supposed to be free to run around. The only way to separate them was to keep one of them in the classroom during playtime, but when Kirsty or Shannon heard her Jaydon had been kept indoors, she came straight round to the school to complain about discrimination against her son. Why should he suffer just because the other was a vile little toe-rag?

'You're f...ing racists!' the two mothers would scream at the teachers, or the first person in authority in the school whom they came across. 'You're only excluding Jaydon because his father's black!'

The teacher, and the rest of the staff, were frightened of Kirsty and Shannon because they said they knew people who would come and sort the school out. They were frightened too because any kind of retaliation, even verbal, would land them in trouble. There was only one good thing about the Jaydons' mothers: they could at least be relied upon not to complain about their sons' lack of progress in reading, writing or arithmetic, as certain pushy mothers did.

Both Jaydons grew quickly, despite an unhealthy diet and a house impregnated with cigarette and other smoke. They learned how to change channels constantly on the cinema-sized screen on the wall at home, watching which was their main occupation when they were not out in the street deliberately crashing their tricycles into people in their path. Kirsty and Shannon competed on their birthdays, by the size of their cakes and the number and expense of their presents to show who loved their Jaydon more. On these occasions, the Jaydons tore the wrappings off the presents with an energy approaching ferocity, but then, strangely, seemed to forget all about the contents almost immediately. Only the debts remained for long, but they could be juggled. No one would take serious legal action against poor single mothers with three children each.

When the Jaydons were six and a half, the school sent a letter to all the parents to tell them that there was going to be a school outing to Filton Towers, a large amusement park about eighty miles away, and asking the parents for a small contribution. 'F...ing cheek!' Kirsty and Shannon both thought. 'I pay my taxes.' Nevertheless, they found the money to pay.

The great day of the outing arrived. It was the first time in their lives that either of the Jaydons had been further than a mile or two from Broadfields Walk. Kirsty and Shannon packed lunches for them – three packets of Cheezy Twists and two bars of Spaceman chocolate for Kirsty's Jaydon, and two packets each of Bacon Monsters and Elephant Chews for Shannon's – and took them to school. Kirsty's Jaydon had a crisis en route: he suddenly decided that he didn't want to go, so Kirsty had to drag him along the road by one arm, kicking and screaming, sometimes lifting him clean off the ground when he managed to dig his heels in. Unlike Graydon, her first-born, he wasn't old or big enough yet to impose his will by physical force.

When they arrived at the school, the bus that was to take them to Filton Towers was parked outside. Kirsty's Jaydon, when he saw it, suddenly forgot that he hadn't wanted to go, broke away from Kirsty, and pushed his way to the head of the queue to get on to the bus.

'Wait, Jaydon, wait,' said one of the teachers. 'Take your turn.' The teacher took Jaydon's hand to lead him to the back of the queue.

'Take your f…ing hand off my son!' shouted Kirsty, rushing forward.

The teacher, startled, released Jaydon, who ran back to the front of the queue.

'What do you think you're f…ing doing?' demanded Kirsty of the teacher.

'Jaydon's got to learn to take his turn,' said the teacher.

'He's only a f…ing kid,' said Kirsty. And she muttered that if she ever caught the teacher laying a hand on her Jaydon again, she would rip her f…ing head off.

Just then, Shannon's Jaydon rushed past her on his way to the head of the queue, brushing her leg.

'Can't you f…ing control your kid?' shouted Kirsty at Shannon.

'Shut your f…ing gob, you fat c…t,' shouted back Shannon. 'Or I'll shut it for you!'

'Who are you calling fat, you fat cow?'

It was true that Shannon weighed a lot more than Kirsty. Another mother intervened.

'Cool it, you two,' she said. 'There are kids here.'

Kirsty and Shannon would have turned on her, but the bus was now ready to go. It moved off. Neither of the Jaydons waved to his mother: they were too busy trying to snatch things from other children or demanding to sit in their seats.

At about three o'clock that afternoon, a policeman appeared

in Broadfields Walk. He was on his own, which was unusual: normally policemen, if they came at all, were in twos or threes at least, and looking more like soldiers than police. They were not a welcome sight in Broadfields Walk.

The policeman knocked at Kirsty's front door. There was no response. He bent down to shout through the flap of the letter box. This wasn't easy for him because his bending movement was stiffened by his stab-proof vest and he was a little portly. He looked a bit like the Michelin Man.

'Open up, police!' he shouted.

There was the sound of three locks being unbolted before the door opened a fraction on a chin. Kirsty's suspicious and hostile face peered out.

'What do you want?' she asked. 'I ain't done nothing wrong. There's no reason for you to come sniffing round here.'

'Mrs Kirsty Ngobo?' asked the policeman. She had briefly been married to an African, but nothing remained of the marriage except the name that she bore for official purposes.

'What if I am?' she replied. As far as she was concerned, the police had only one aim or purpose in life: to pin something on you. Even when you'd done it, they made up the evidence.

'I'm afraid I've got some bad news,' he said, in a tone to which she was completely unaccustomed, not only in policemen.

'Can I come in?' asked the policeman.

Kirsty realised that it must be something serious (unlike a suspected crime committed by her latest boyfriend) because this was not the way policemen usually spoke to her.

'If you must,' said Kirsty, still mistrustfully. 'But I'm very busy.'

'I won't take much of your time,' said the policeman, stepping inside as he took his helmet off. 'I'm P.C. Roberts, but you can call me Bob. That's what everyone else calls me.'

His familiarity did not reassure Kirsty. It sounded false.

'I think you should sit down,' he said to her. Then he suggested that she turn the television off, and she complied by turning the sound down so that it was almost inaudible.

'I want you to stay calm,' said the policeman. 'I'm afraid there's been a terrible accident.'

'Accident? What accident?'

'The school bus.'

'What do you mean?'

'The bus veered off the road and hit a tree. The driver was trying to avoid an oncoming vehicle, and swerved to the left.' The policeman, now sitting, revolved his helmet in his hands. 'There were injuries. I'm sorry to say your Jaydon was among them. In fact... in fact... he is... he is dead.'

There was a momentary silence, as if Kirsty could not take in what he had said. Then she let out a shriek and began keening.

'I'm very sorry,' said the policeman.

Kirsty came to herself.

'Sorry? Is that all you can f...ing say, and Jaydon dead! I've lost a son and you're sorry?'

'I can't tell you...'

What couldn't he tell her? How awkward he felt? That he'd much rather be arresting someone? That he had another call with the same news to tell?

He got up to go.

'I must be getting on,' he said. 'Here,' he continued, taking something from inside his vest and holding it out for her to take. It was a pamphlet titled *What to Do When You Have Lost a Loved One*. On the cover was a picture of an old man and woman, the woman sitting and the man standing with his hand on her shoulder. 'It has practical hints...'

Kirsty flung it away. The policeman picked it up and handed it back to her. People often reacted like that at first, especially the kind of people who lived in Broadfields Walk, but later they were pleased of it. He expected the same reaction when he went with similar news to Shannon's flat, and he was right. Still, it was wearing on the nerves.

Although other children had been injured in the crash, the two Jaydons were the only ones killed. Their mothers' grief gave way to anger when their bodies were not released for burial, as the coroner's office put it, until the pathologist had had completed his post mortem on them. Unfortunately, there was a backlog of cases, due to budgetary cuts; and he, the pathologist, was snowed under. Anyway, what did they need a post mortem for? Wasn't it f…ing obvious what Jaydon had died of? He – they - had been flung through the windscreen of the bus when it hit the tree. What more did the f…ing coroner want? Wasn't it f…ing obvious?

Shannon's Jaydon was released first for burial, so his funeral came first. There was a large turnout at the local cemetery for the interment. Local feeling ran high about the accident: it was as if the local school didn't care about the children. When the headmistress appeared at the graveside to represent the school, she was jeered, jostled and insulted.

'We don't need no crocodile tears,' one of the women present, also a mother, shouted. 'We need action.'

Even the women from Orchard Meadow, the cul-de-sac round the corner from Broadfields Walk, who usually thought themselves a cut above because their boyfriends could park their cars in their concreted-over front gardens instead of on the street, showed their solidarity by shouting at the headmistress. Who did she think she was, coming here when it was all her fault? When she scurried away, they whistled at her.

There were so many bouquets of flowers delivered to the cemetery that the sexton and undertaker had to move several piles of them to find the place of interment that had already been dug. The teddy bears were also a nuisance and got in the way. You had to be careful not to tread on them, let alone kick them aside, because mistreating a teddy bear was just like abusing a child. You had to treat them solicitously, like a child. One of the teddy bears, sent by someone who felt Jaydon's death particularly strongly, was four feet high.

'Watch that teddy!' someone shouted, when the undertaker accidentally knocked it in the direction of the grave-to-be.

'It's Jaydon we're burying,' someone shouted back. 'Not some f…ing teddy bear.' There was a guffaw from somewhere within the crowd, followed by 'Shut your mouth! Show some f...ing respect!'

During the ceremony, Shannon sobbed so much that she almost had to be held up, or she might have slipped to the ground (which was muddy because it had rained overnight). Several of the mourners took videos of her on their phones which later they posted on their sites, as well as pictures of themselves, which numbers of their friends indicated that they liked. When the ceremony was over, Shannon felt strangely deflated. She still had two other children to microwave meals for because they were too idle to do it for themselves.

It was Kirsty's turn three days later. She had heard about Shannon's Jaydon's ceremony via the Broadfields Walk telegraph which, as usual, was very efficient if not always disinterestedly so. She was determined that her Jaydon's ceremony should be bigger, with more flowers and accoutrements such as plastic windmills, that Sannon's Jaydon's had been. Early on, she had decided on jet-black helium balloons with Jaydon's name printed on them in gold lettering, to be released at the end of the ceremony. Initially, she had wanted *Fly with the angels* printed on them also, but she was told it as not worth the expense: no one would be able to read it once the balloons were more than a few feet up in the air. The same effect would be created just by the balloons themselves.

The two Jaydons were buried next to one another.

But the inquests into their deaths took many months to arrange: there was no explanation why. First came the inquest touching, as the archaic language put it, the death of Kirsty's Jaydon because, having been flung out of the bus before Shannon's Jaydon, he was deemed to have died first.

'Touching?' exclaimed Kirsty, when she first had notice of the inquest. 'What are they, a bunch of f...ing paedos, or what?'

The corner was a tall, thin, elderly man with a grey toothbrush moustache: one might have thought he was a retired colonel of the old school. When he spoke, it was as if he found words distasteful to him. He thought they should be used with precision, or not at all. Unnecessary words were a kind of pollution.

Kirsty had retained a lawyer. Since Jaydon's death must have been someone's fault, there must also have been compensation in it. It wasn't the money that Kirsty was after, of course, it was just that she wanted to make sure that no one else ever suffered what she had been through.

Her lawyer at the inquest was a refined young lady of Indian origin who wanted to make her way in the law. It was her job to procure from the coroner a verdict of death by negligence, which would make the subsequent task of suing for damages all the easier. But who should be sued? The school, being public-ly-funded, had (at least potentially) the most money: but on the other hand, the bus company and its insurance company was more likely to give in quickly from fear of the costs of litigation.

The corner emphasised that the purpose of the inquest was simply and solely to determine what had happened and not to apportion blame, but everyone knew this to be a lie, if some knew it to be a noble one. It was perfectly obvious what killed Jaydon, plus or minus a broken bone or two. The purpose of the inquest was to find who was at fault.

The witness for whom everyone waited was the bus driver. Before him, the pathologist had spoken in a dry, matter-of-fact way. For him, even the corpse of a child was only material for work, like wood for a carpenter. His evidence was laden with jargon that most people in the court did not understand. He was as comfortable in the witness-box as a dog in its basket. It was one of his natural environments.

The bus driver, by contrast, was nervous. He had never ap-peared in a court before. He was fat, one of those drivers whose stomach, when he sat at the wheel, might seem to interfere with his ability to turn the wheel. Almost any physical effort or movement seemed to wring sweat from him, and he kept dab-bing at his face and forehead with his handkerchief. This made him appear guilty, though he was not an accused. Even the three steps up to the witness-box had made him breathless. All in all, everyone was prepared not to believe him, not because of what he said, but because of how he was.

His evidence started tamely enough, with neutral questions

about the time he had gone to work, what he had had for breakfast, how long he had been a bus driver, and so on, but eventually it came to the moments before the crash.

'Them kids,' he said, 'was running up and down the bus between the seats. I kept telling them to sit down and so did the teacher, but they wouldn't take no notice of us. I told them that if they didn't sit down I would have to stop the bus. I didn't want to be responsible for what happened if I had to brake sudden.' The driver, obviously distressed at the memory, began a general lament. 'The trouble with kids these days,' he said, 'is that you can't tell them nothing. If you do, they just cheek you. In my day, if you spoke to a grown-up like that you got a clip round the ear that soon put you right.'

'Thank you, Mr Smith,' interrupted the coroner. 'Please just answer the questions.'

Well, them kids (as Mr Smith put it) had been running up and down the bus like banshees, distracting him constantly. It was hard enough to drive a bus without that kind of thing, what with the traffic these days. Then some lunatic on the other side of the road…

At this point Kirsty stood up and started to scream at the driver.

'Lies! All lies! You're a liar!'

The coroner, startled for a moment, called for order. He asked Kirsty to sit down, but she took no notice.

'He's a liar! He's trying to blame my Jaydon, to say it was all his fault! He's saying it's my Jaydon that made him crash! But is wasn't. It was because he was too fat and lazy to brake properly. Look at him! He killed my Jaydon!'

She began to sob very loudly. Her lawyer, who was sitting in front of her, turned to try to comfort, or at least to calm, her. She was too well-dressed to bring Kirsty any comfort. Kirsty brushed her efforts aside: she didn't need no help from a stuck-up Paki lawyer. Kirsty managed to control her sobs enough to shout 'Murderer! Murderer!' at the driver.

The coroner said he would adjourn the court for fifteen minutes for Kirsty to compose herself. During this break, Kirsty expostulated with her lawyer, the useless bitch. Why did she just sit there during the driver's lies? She wasn't paying her just to sit there to say nothing (not that Kirsty was paying her), like a f… ing stuffed dummy. The lawyer tried to explain to her that there was an order and procedure that she had to follow, and that her time would come to ask questions, but Kirsty just said, 'Don't give me none of that!' Her tears of anger had made a terrible mess of her mascara. The lawyer advised her to go to the toilets to clean up the dried rivulets of black that had run down her cheeks.

'Where are they?' Kirsty asked, and the lawyer pointed to them. On the way, Kirsty muttered 'He's lying! He's a liar.'

The hearing resumed and the bus driver climbed back into the witness box as if it were a Himalaya. He was reminded that he was still on oath. He had been shaken by Kirsty's outburst and his voice was tremulous.

'As I said,' he continued when the same question as before was put to him by the coroner, 'this lunatic on the other side of the road tried to overtake on a bend and…'

Kirsty rose up again.

'This is a f…ing farce!' she shouted, and stormed out of the court. Her high heels clicked on the parquet floor. She had put on her best shoes for Jaydon.

The court was nonplussed for a moment. How to proceed? Kirsty's lawyer, however, said that she would continue to represent Kirsty, as she had not been formally dismissed as her legal adviser. The coroner thanked her, but although there was a clearing of the atmosphere after Kirsty's departure, there was a feeling to the proceedings of pointlessness and anti-climax afterwards. When Kirsty's lawyer had finished asking the bus driver questions – when he had had his last medical check-up, his eyes tested, and so forth, and why he had not stopped the vehicle by the roadside until the children behaved themselves, for after all it was the adults who were in charge of the children, not the other way round – the court usher approached the bus driver as he was climbing laboriously out of the witness-box and advised him that it might be best if he left the court by the rear door, because you never knew these days who might be waiting for him at the front, Kirsty might have arranged for some of her friends etc., etc. The bus driver took the usher's advice.

The inquest on Shannon's Jaydon followed soon after that on Kirsty's Jaydon, but Shannon did not attend because she had just started with Courtney, who was not fond of involvement with courts, not even at second hand. In any case, nothing different emerged.

It took a little while for both Kirsty and Shannon to find and erect tombstones in the cemetery. They each tried to find out, through mutual acquaintances, what the other was planning to erect. They both wanted their Jaydon's tombstone to be better, more noticeable, than the other's. This desire made it difficult for them to choose and stick to their choice: but eventually they had to take the risk, and plump for one or another. They tried to find out from the undertaker what the other had chosen, but he said that he was bound by professional and commercial secrecy, and refused to tell them.

In the end, Shannon chose something that was now common, if not quite traditional: a heart-shaped stone of shiny black granite, inscribed with a short poem chosen from a catalogue of such verses:

My little angel's gone to play
In the fields above the sky
Where it's always sunny day
And greatest joy can never die.

Ideally, Shannon would have like a second verse, but the undertaker advised her that one verse was more effective than two, besides which the cost of the extra engraving and gold lettering would have been prohibitive.

Underneath the poem were inscribed the words:

Goodnight Jaydon. Sweet dreams.

Kirsty, as was only to be expected, chose something much

more adventurous and original. She chose a perfectly round slab of the same black granite, carved like a football. The inscription was simple:

My little footballer Jaydon
Who one day would have played for Man. United

Underneath was an engraving of a man in football kit kicking a ball.

There was no doubting Kirsty's victory over Shannon in the tombstone competition. Kirsty was exultant for a moment, mocking Shannon to her friends, but then began to worry about Shannon's revenge. She wouldn't take it lying down. What form would her revenge take? Damaging the actual tombstone might be difficult; it was of granite, after all, and granite wasn't called granite for nothing. More likely it would consist of damaging or removing the objects which she had placed round the grave to show how much she had loved her Jaydon. And of course she had noticed that as soon as she had put something new such as a fresh plastic windmill or a plaster squirrel round her Jaydon's grave, a bigger plastic windmill or plaster squirrel (or badger) would appear round Shannon's Jaydon's grave. Even worse were the football scarves: when Kirsty tied one round the tombstone in Manchester United colours, Shannon would tie one round her Jaydon's tombstone in Manchester City colours. Bitch! Couldn't she think up anything for herself?

Of course, tying a Manchester City scarf round her Jaydon's tomb was a declaration of war. Well, if she wanted a war, she could have one.

In any case, it was absurd to compare the two Jaydons when it came to football. Her Jaydon – Kirsty's, that is – had been gifted from the moment he found a ball at his feet, unlike her Jaydon – Shannon's, that is – who was as likely to trip over it as kick it, and certainly never in the direction he wanted. To mention them in the same breath was not only absurd but an insult. In a fury of indignation, Kirsty tore the scarf from Shannon's Jaydon's tombstone, and trampled it into the mud. Who did Shannon think she was?

Of course, retaliation as not long in coming, but even in retaliation Shannon showed herself to be imitative. She, or one of her friends (if she had any) tore the Manchester United scarf from Kirsty's Jaydon's tombstone. She did show just a touch of originality, however. Having trodden it into the ground, she (or whoever it was) put some dog poo on it.

There followed a combat of spray paint, which had to be removed. It was lucky they had both chosen highly-polished stone, for think how difficult it would have been to remove spray paint from absorbent stone! Kirsty found some extra-indelible canary yellow paint with which she inscribed the words *Mother is a slut* on Shannon's Jaydon's tombstone. It took Shannon hours to clean it off.

From now on it was tit-for-tat. First all the plastic flowers and plastic pot plants went; then the sodden teddy bears, their fur grey with sun and rain and earth. But Kirsty, ever the more inventive of the two, left one teddy leaning against Shannon's Jaydon's tombstone: but with its glass, or plastic, eyes pulled out. Shannon screamed when she saw it. She took some stones and spelt the word BARSTERD with them next to Kirsty's Jaydon's grave.

Finally, Shannon, or one of her friends, overstepped the mark: the inscription on Kirsty's Jaydon's tombstone was badly damaged with a portable drill. It would cost a fortune to restore it, if it could be done at all, and Kirsty was already maxed out on her cards, as she put it.

By chance, Kirsty ran into Shannon on the day the damage was inflicted on the tombstone. The bitch was pregnant again and proud of it, as if she'd done something clever. Anyone could see that Courtney, the baby-father, would f... off the day the baby was born, if not before.

'You f...ing stupid cow!' screamed Kirsty when she saw Shannon in the street.

'F...ing stupid cow yourself!' replied Shannon.

'You f...ing damaged Jaydon's grave.'

'I never laid a f...ing finger on it! It's not even worth damaging.'

Kirsty flew at her. She grabbed her by the hair, wrestled her to the ground and banged her head on it as hard as she could. She left her lying there, having taught her a lesson she would not forget in a long time.

At first, she claimed she had acted in self-defence, but her lawyer advised her to change her story and think of something else when the post mortem showed that Shannon's head had been smashed on the ground many times, repeatedly, and it was the opinion of the neurologist that she must have been unconscious at the time many of the blows were inflicted. At first Kirsty couldn't grasp that this meant she couldn't have been acting in self-defence, but eventually she understood. At her lawyer's suggestion, she then went for provocation which had caused her temporarily to lose her mind, so that she hadn't known what she was doing. Her lawyer advised her to express remorse, which she did.

She said that Shannon had screamed at her across the road that her (Kirsty's) Jaydon had been the one to cause the crash and if she had brought him up properly her (Shannon's) Jaydon would still be alive: but if her (Kirsty's) Jaydon had survived, he wouldn't have played for Manchester United, he would have spent his life in prison, his mother being such a slut. Anyone would have seen red if spoken to like that.

When she had repeated her story two or three times, she came to believe it, and even grew indignant at the recollection of it. But there was no one to corroborate it, and at her trial no one believed it. A psychiatrist said that her unresolved grief for her Jaydon had made her vulnerable to violence, that is to say, likely to commit it.

When she was sentenced, she screamed at the judge that he was a stuck-up c...t, and didn't know what he was f...ing talking about. He didn't know what it was to lose a child.

FILIAL PIETY

ROGER, FELIX AND DAVID (all of them divorced, Roger twice) were three brothers, the sons of Mrs. Marsh of Harton Hall, a Georgian mansion in the country. Though they had been expensively educated, they were all, in their own way, failures. Roger was a drunkard, Felix was a gambler, and David called himself a poet though he had never published anything nor ever would. Mrs Marsh's friends, in the days when she still had some, used to say between them with sorrowful pleasure that the boys' expectations had ruined them: that had they been obliged to make their way in the world they would have made more of themselves.

Mrs Marsh was a rich widow, now ancient, and her husband had left the sons an annual allowance, enough to live on, but not enough to live on well, according to their own lights. They each of them declined to increase their income by consistent effort, preferring to await their inheritance and in the meantime coast along without serious effort.

The main problem with this plan of life was that Mrs Marsh stubbornly refused to die. In fact she was seldom ill and clung on to life like a limpet to a rock. She was frail, it is true, but one does not die of frailty. She was so old now that her boys were approaching old age themselves. There was therefore bitterness towards her in their hearts. Her failure to die was a symptom of

27

her lack of consideration for them, which they began to project in their memories back to their childhood, when she packed them off to school as soon as she could. All the same, they still called her Mummy, and David sometimes called her Mumsy.

Mrs Marsh now needed assistance to live: and a lot of it. In addition to the housekeeper she had always had, she employed a relay team of four nurses whom she insisted upon calling, and thinking of, as cleaning ladies. They were all black, three from Africa and one from the West Indies, and unfortunately, before she needed them, Mrs Marsh had never held with Africans or their descendants. Sometimes, when her dementia got the better of her and overcame the rather distant politeness instilled in her as a child as part of the *quid pro quo* for having been of gentle birth, she would call them jungle bunnies. Fortunately they laughed it off, and said that it was her illness that was talking. All old ladies were like that; besides, at other times she showed herself considerate and almost affectionate towards them, even if she could never quite remember who they were.

Her memory for almost everything less than fifty years ago had gone, leaving behind certain aspects of her character like the grin of the Cheshire Cat, such as the expectation of being obeyed and having her wishes fulfilled by others as if they were as important to them as they were to her. Her impatience of delay therefore remained, but it was now combined with an anxiety born of slight awareness that something was wrong. At first she had known that the problem was her memory, but now she could not put her finger on what it was and all that remained was a disturbing awareness that all was not right.

She had a list by her of numbers to call in case of emergency. Unfortunately, she no longer knew what an emergency was: or rather, because of her loss of understanding, everything was now an emergency. She had only to feel a little more anxious than usual to call one of her sons, but increasingly she forgot that she had called the same son only moments before. Unreassured, she forgot that she had been reassured moments before.

She would say that she was not feeling well. The son she had called would ask her in what way she was not feeling well. She would say that she had a headache and must have had a stroke. The son would say she could not have had a stroke, otherwise she would not have been able to call. She would grow angry, and say that her son did not understand or care what happened to her. Then he would ask her whether she would like him to call a doctor for her. Then she would grow scornful. What could a doctor do for her? Then he would ask her, in that case, what she wanted him to do for her. She would say that she wanted one of her children to come to her. He would say that he would be there within the hour. Although this was not soon enough for her, it would assuage her somewhat. He had no intention of coming, of course, and she would soon forget the promise and telephone a few minutes later, when exactly the same conversation (if it could be called that) would ensue. She had been known to call fifty times a day, and in the end her sons told the carers to disconnect the telephone. The carers, who were a little afraid of Mrs March in her more imperious moods, and who in any case had a respect rather than a disdain for old age, asked what they should say to her when the phone went dead. 'Anything you like,' they replied: she wouldn't remember or know whether or not it was plausible. There had been a storm and the lines were down, flooding, lightning, anything they liked, even a terrorist attack on the exchange. The good thing about someone else's memory loss was that liars no longer had to have good memories. The only purpose of saying anything was to calm her down.

At first her sons visited her regularly, but their visits became fewer and fewer. What was the point of them, in fact? True, she would express some, usually slightly sour and disapproving, pleasure at their arrival, but as soon as they were gone she forgot that they had ever come. It was surely not worth the effort to produce pleasure that was so slight, fleeting and so soon forgotten. It may have been that to others they seemed to live lives of leisure, but to themselves they seemed very busy. There was always some lunch to attend, some form to be studied, some line of poetry to be wrestled over. And Harton Hall was undoubtedly out of the way, a most inconvenient place to reach.

The house was also completely inappropriate to the old lady's needs and comfort. She should not have been living on her own (the staff counted as nobody). Though she moved very little and never without assistance, they thought of her as rattling about the house like a dried pea in a drum. This image in their minds was strengthened by the fact that she had shrunken, shrivelled and desiccated in her person. She was now half the size she had once been, so that now her imperiousness seemed to be like a distillation. Her old social charm (she had been an accomplished hostess, and had been presented at court) remained, but only intermittently. Fortunately, she soon forgot the orders that she had given and so could not be angered by non-fulfilment of them, as she would once have been, but she always had others to issue.

The proper upkeep of the house had always been very expensive, but now it was decaying from neglect. The gutters blocked with dead leaves and caused damp to seep through the walls; rooms went unheated and began to smell of mould. Paint flaked from window-frames and sash windows ceased to work. Weeds grew in the garden because the gardener who came twice a week was now old, could hardly bend down and was completely unsupervised. There was an air of ruination about Harton Hall.

It would have cost a fortune to put right and the three sons, to whom Mrs Marsh had been persuaded by an old family solicitor to grant powers of attorney before it was too late (a step she had been reluctant to take because she said that she knew what her sons were like), could see no point in wasting money in this fashion. The upkeep of the Hall was quite enough as it was, without repair; their mother would not notice the difference if the Hall were spick and span; and none of the brothers proposed to live at the Hall after her death. It would be bought by a very rich man who would easily have the means to restore it; the costs of doing so before sale would be greater than the sale value added to the house.

The sons, who were not close, met from time to time to discuss their mother's affairs and situation, by which they meant the state of their inheritance. The wages of the staff to look after her were eating into her capital, being greater than her income, the very capital on which their expectations were founded. It was Felix, who had long had the habit of borrowing quite large sums from his mother without paying them back, who first brought up the subject at one of their meetings.

'At this rate,' he said, 'she'll run out of money in ten to twelve years.'

Roger, who had driven to the meeting drunk, and had consumed another whisky on his arrival ('I always drive better after a few,' he said), pointed out that it was very unlikely that she would live that long.

David, the bohemian of the family, suddenly turned actuary, and said lugubriously, 'She might.' The prospect pleased none of them very much.

The question, then, was how to stem the haemorrhage of money before it ran out. It was impossible while she was at the Hall to dispense with the staff. Though she frequently objected to their presence, demanding to know who they were and why they were there, and imagining them to be intruders bent on stealing her things, including her spectacles and the *Daily Telegraph* that she claimed still to read though she never did, the blackness of their complexions only adding to her suspicions (she had never invited a black person into her house in her life, and indeed would not have spoken to one to invite), she could not tolerate being alone for a moment. If left on her own even briefly, she turned at once to the telephone, and panicked when it seemed not to work. Then she knew that burglars had cut the wires. If by some chance the telephone was not disconnected, her sons would not answer, also causing her to panic. She would work her way desperately down the list of numbers, like a woman possessed, starting again from the top once she had reached the bottom. When the nurse returned, she would demand to know who she was and with whose permission she had entered her house. Sometimes she would even take her stick, leaning against the side of her chair, and hit out to defend herself from the intruder.

'This can't go on,' said Felix. 'She's on the phone all the time, she panics...'

'She can't be happy like that,' said Roger, gloomy and rheumy-eyed.

'I wonder whether the time has come...' said David.

'For her own good...'

The two others had understood perfectly what David meant: they had discussed it before. She wasn't happy at home and once, when Felix had visited unexpectedly, he had found her arm covered in bruises. The nurse on duty said it was from falls the night before, but they had all read in the newspapers stories of abuse of the elderly by carers. It wouldn't be at all surprising if, exasperated beyond endurance by her arrogance and inclination to disparagement, one of the nurses had lost her temper and struck her or pulled her about. Older people bruise easily, after all, and even Roger, more than twenty years younger than she, had noticed that he bruised more easily than he used to when he knocked into things. The next thing they would hear was that she had fallen and broken her hip, allegedly by having fallen out of bed. It was time to move her for safety's sake. It would have the secondary advantage of being far, far cheaper.

'There are some very good homes,' said Felix.

'If she were nearer us, we could visit her more often,' said David.

'She would be happier,' said Roger. 'Or at least, better looked after...'

'We'll have to do some research,' said Felix. 'Not all homes are good.'

'Some are,' said Roger, with an air of profundity that having drunk too much gives some people.

'Yes, some,' said Felix. 'Some being the operative word. Some are very good.'

But which of them would actually do the necessary research? Roger was unreliable and David other-worldly. Besides, it would bore them to do it. Felix was the obvious choice – he was at least conscientious in his choice of horses on which to bet – and, reluctantly, he agreed to look into it.

'Make sure it's value for money,' said Roger, who had never been known to economise before.

Then David had a disturbing idea, or question.

'How do we get her there when we've found it?'

True, it was a problem. She hadn't been out of the Hall for at least three years. She was extremely frail: when you moved her, you felt as if you had a very fine piece of porcelain in your hands that could easily break into fragments. And what would they tell her when they fetched her away, never to return?

'We've never taken her anywhere before,' said David.

'That doesn't matter,' said Felix. 'She won't remember. We can tell her anything. We can tell her that we're taking her on her weekly outing, like last week and every week. She won't know any different. There are some advantages to a shot memory.'

Indeed, sometimes she feigned having remembered something she had just been told to cover up the fact that she could remember nothing of the last forty years or more. She was not the kind of woman to take humiliation without a struggle.

'We could tell her the home was a hotel,' said Roger, his limited imagination now stirred. 'With a spa. After all, Mummy used to go to Carlsbad every year before the war.'

'Which war was that, Roger?' asked Felix, who knew that Roger's grasp of the past was weak. And with his drinking, he was next in line for amnesia. 'I think you mean Baden.'

Nevertheless, they would have to tell her something along the lines Roger suggested, something like 'It will only be for a short time, a rest will do you good, the doctor ordered it.' That would allow them to slip away before she turned awkward. And they could say the same thing every time they saw her, for as long as she lasted.

Felix, then, was the one deputed to find a home. David's head was in the clouds, Roger's hand on the bottle. Felix's obsessiveness and attention to detail was what was needed. But of course the others would want to be fully informed, especially as to price, before they gave their approval. Felix was quite capable of double invoicing when it came to it.

Felix alighted on Edentrees, a home in a former mansion

approached through a park with an avenue of ancient trees. The entrance hall was just what was needed to create a favourable impression on someone like Mrs Marsh: through Doric columns into a large expanse of parquet leading to a sweeping staircase. A couple of Eighteenth Century portraits of middling quality and a splendid chandelier completed the satisfactory cadre.

The dining room was equally satisfactory. It could almost have been a hotel in pre-war Carlsbad. There was snowy linen and silverware aplenty; only a faint acrid smell of urine, so difficult to remove once it has impregnated a room, spoiled the impression. But it was unimportant: Mrs Marsh had almost lost her sense of smell and of taste. If she sometimes complained about the food put before her, it was more for form's sake than anything else.

Her bedroom-to-be was rather less satisfactory, but there would be no need to show it her before she moved in or before Felix, who had also been deputed to take her, had deposited her in Edentrees. In fact, her bedroom was in a modern wing attached to the old house, cunningly concealed from view as you approached it. The room was comfortable enough but without character, like that in an airport hotel; even the hunting prints on the walls could not disguise its impersonality. There was something absurd about the instructions about what to do in case of fire that was hung on the door. The residents would have to be rescued or burnt to a crisp: that was all. But regulations are regulations, and have to be obeyed.

There was nothing too alarming about the few residents of Edentrees whom Felix observed in the public rooms: in the dining room and what was called the writing room. There were a few old ladies in wheelchairs pushed by gratifyingly European, if not quite English, staff; the old ladies were well-dressed and coiffed, with pearl necklaces or earrings, even if they did smell a little of incontinence. Edentrees was evidently a superior establishment, certainly superior to the other home, Greenacres, that Felix had visited, which consisted of two semi-detached houses knocked together, abutting a main road with concreted-over front gardens for parking, presided over by a fat Mauritian couple. In Greenacres, the old women sat round the edge of a dayroom like eternal wallflowers at a dance, while the television relayed keep-fit programmes.

'Dr Elliott is our medical adviser,' said the Matron of Edentrees to Felix in her office. 'A most experienced man.'

The Matron had called for tea, and it arrived on a silver tray in an elegant china teapot.

'He inspires the greatest confidence,' resumed the Matron. 'Our guests and just as important, our guests' relatives, are very happy with him.' She went on to explain that, at Edentrees, the guests could have as much or as little social contact with each other just as they wished, and could take their meals either in their rooms or in the dining room. Furthermore, meals could be served to visiting friends and relatives, although at extra cost; Edentrees prided itself on its cuisine, simple but balanced and nourishing. Moreover, if anyone wanted anything in particular or, of course, had special dietary requirements...

'Is there a place available?' asked Felix.

'Not just at the moment,' said the Matron. 'But we're expecting one to become available at any moment. Mrs Frith-Roberts...' Matron's voice trailed away.

This answer was, like Edentrees itself, highly satisfactory: and, surprisingly, the home was not vastly more expensive that Greenacres had been. The Matron promised to notify Felix as soon as a place – *the* place, in fact – became available.

The day came for the removal of Mrs Marsh from Harton Hall to Edentrees.

'Come on Mummy,' said Felix. 'We're going for a ride.'

'A ride?' said Mrs Marsh suspiciously.

'Yes, like the one we go on every Tuesday.'

Mrs Marsh did not like to admit that she did not remember that they went on a ride every Tuesday.

'Oh yes,' she said.

'It gets you out of the house,' elaborated Felix. 'You don't want to be stuck indoors all the time, do you?'

Edentrees was three quarters of an hour away from the Hall.

During the journey, Mrs Marsh stared ahead out of the window without any curiosity. Only once did she ask where they were going.

'A surprise, Mummy,' said Felix, as if speaking to a child. But most of the time she seemed hardly aware that they were going anywhere, that they had a destination.

The Matron met them at Edentrees as they drew up.

'Here we are,' said Felix.

'Where?' asked Mrs Marsh.

'Edentrees Royal Hotel and Spa,' said Felix. 'You're here for a little break and a rest. The word 'rest' turned briefly into dust in Felix's mouth: rest from what? She had not exerted herself for years, in fact she had never exerted herself. Everything had always been done for. Apart from the inconvenience of giving birth, she had been entirely spoilt.

'Just for a fortnight,' said Felix. 'Until you're feeling a little better. You haven't been well recently.'

Again, Mrs Marsh did not like to admit she could not remember feeling unwell. Even she knew that it was not completely implausible.

'Welcome to Edentrees,' said the Matron, as Mrs Marsh was helped out of the car like a breech delivery. A nurse behind the Matron smiled and nodded. Felix thought, 'At least it isn't raining.'

Between Felix and the Matron, they guided Mrs Marsh into the building. Once inside, Mrs Marsh swept her stick round the entrance hall and demanded to know where this was and why they were here. There was disdain in her voice, which Felix thought a bit rich after the decrepitude of Harton Hall. Edentrees was in an immaculate state of repair.

'Edentrees, Mummy,' said Felix. 'Royal Hotel and Spa. The Queen Mother stayed here once. You're here for a few days' rest. You've been a bit peaky lately – overdoing it.'

'I feel perfectly fine,' said Mrs Marsh with asperity. 'There's nothing wrong with me.'

An assistant brought up a wheelchair. It was some way to her room, obviously further than she could walk.

'Here, Mummy, sit in the chair,' said Felix helpfully. 'You'll be more comfortable.'

'No I won't. I don't need that thing. Take it away.' She struck it with her stick.

But between the nurse and the assistant, she was manoeuvred into the chair. The Matron drew Felix aside.

'They're all like that to begin with,' she assured him. 'They soon settle down. So long as they don't try to escape, they have given implied consent.'

'Implied consent?'

'Yes, when they don't have legal capacity to decide for themselves,' said the Matron. 'We can keep them as long as we need because they're not trying to leave.'

'Until… until…?' said Felix, interrogatively but vaguely. The Matron knew what he meant.

'Precisely,' she said firmly, 'though we hope not. But we're prepared for that as well. We have a chaplain who visits regularly and is on call. Or a priest if you like.'

'Oh, I hardly think that'll be necessary,' said Felix. 'Mummy's not like that, never has been.'

The Matron nodded. It was a bit of a relief, frankly. Religion interfered with routine, and nothing was more important for running a good home than routine.

'I think you can go now and leave your mother in our hands,' said the Matron, noticing a slight agitation on Felix's part. 'The longer you stay, the more disturbed she'll be when you go. We can manage her safely. She'll settle down. If she doesn't, Dr Elliott is very good.'

Felix was only too happy to take the Matron at her word. She obviously knew what she was doing.

'Goodbye, Mummy,' he said airily to Mrs Marsh, who was now glaring glumly from the wheelchair. 'I'll visit you soon. So will Roger and David.' Of that he was not quite sure, but he said it anyway.

The three brothers, however, did meet again soon. The most urgent thing was to dismiss the staff to staunch the bleeding of funds.

'I'll give them a month's notice,' said Felix.

'Do we have to give them notice?' asked Roger. 'After all, they're not doing a thing now that Mummy's not there.'

'Yes, we do,' said Felix. 'I think it's the law, but I'll check if you like.'

'They've been with us a long time,' said David.

'Don't be sentimental, David,' said Roger. 'They've probably been robbing us blind all that time. If you really feel like that, give them your own money.'

Like the others, David didn't have any of his own money to give, or at least none that he could spare.

Then there was the question of what to do with Harton Hall. David, fresh from his moral defeat over the dismissal of the staff, said it would fetch more if it were restored, but the others told him that he was a poet, he had no grasp of business matters.

'Don't be ridiculous, David,' said Felix. 'It would cost a fortune to make any real difference. It would use up all of Mummy's capital. And it'd delay the sale by months or years, while we would still have to pay the bills. What we need to do is sell the bally place.'

None of them had much sentimental attachment to the Hall, perhaps because Mrs Marsh had not found the task of bringing them up in it very interesting and had deputed it to nannies (all now dead) and schools. During the holidays, the brothers had been packed off on supposedly improving jaunts to learn foreign languages that they had never mastered and would never master. Thus even the Hall's grounds, which might otherwise have been a paradise to small boys, meant little to them.

Despite its decrepitude, Felix (again it was he) managed to sell the Hall at an advantageous price to a local building contractor, the illegitimate son of a charwoman, who had great plans for it: to turn the library into a private cinema, for example.

The third question to be resolved was what to do with Mummy's money in the meantime. The stock market was high and therefore a risk, but interest rates were low and merely depositing the money would yield very little. Preserving the capital (the all-important goal) while deriving an income to pay for Edentrees would not be easy. Edentrees, while cheaper than keeping Mummy at home, was not cheap.

'We need capital growth,' said Roger.

'But at no risk,' said David unpoetically.

This was a circle that was difficult to square. They agreed on a compromise between Felix who would have put the money on the stock market like he would have thrown the dice on the gaming table, and David who would have played safe and been prepared to watch the money slowly eaten away in the hope that it would not be for long. They did a little of both. If the stock market fell, they would still have some ready cash. If it rose, they would make a profit. But all three of them thought of the money as already theirs, with only a temporary obstacle to its enjoyment.

'Anyway,' said Felix brightly, 'it won't be for long.'

'What do you mean?' asked David, pretending that the thought had never occurred to him.

Felix, who was professionally interested, as it were, in the question of odds, had looked up how long, statistically-speaking, a woman of Mrs Marsh's age could be expected to survive. It was about three years if she stayed at home, less than six months, and more like three, if she was in a nursing home.

'A year or two at the most,' said Felix, settling on an average.

Mentally, they divided the remaining assets by three, after they had deducted the tax. They wouldn't be rich – not like Mummy had always been – but their financial anxieties would be relieved, at least for a time.

The problem, however, was that Mummy did not die as quickly as expected. This did not mean that she had settled down at Edentrees, or was happy and contented there. She had often to be coaxed, begged, cajoled, or bullied into getting up, washing herself or eating. Sometimes she shut her eyes as if by doing so she banished the world; sometimes she groaned as if she had been run over by a bus; sometimes, more peremptorily, she demanded to be left in peace, using language that once would never have escaped her lips. When food was placed before her, she would push it away and clamp her mouth shut like a small child in front of a plate of spinach; she said she had no appetite, could not eat and that swallowing was impossible for her. Food disgusted her, it nauseated her to eat, she said, was like slavery; a form of forced labour. Once cajoled or bullied into eating a few mouthfuls, however, her capacity was surprising, especially for things like ice-cream that please children, and she lost no weight, often a sign of impending death among the residents of Edentrees. Needless to say, it was pointless to draw attention to the contradiction between her previous claims not to be hungry or her inability to swallow and her subsequent performance: she had neither sufficient memory nor capacity for logical thought. No moment of her life had any connection with any other moment.

Her three sons visited her rarely, even less frequently than they had visited her at the Hall. As far as they could tell, their visits brought her no pleasure, rather the reverse, which came as a relief to them because it justified their infrequency. They saw her obstinacy when food was brought to her and assumed that she behaved this way for their 'benefit', to gain their attention or make them feel guilty: that would be just like her, how she had always been. Sometimes, when she was in one of her rare good moods, she would tell them how she had been out shopping that morning for their Christmas presents. The necessity not to contradict an obvious untruth never failed to create a tension in their minds. It is difficult to listen to obvious untruths without saying anything.

Their visits became ever-fewer and briefer: they made occasional telephone enquiries. They hoped for news, but it was a long time coming. Why was she lingering? Her life was pointless. It was selfish of her to cling on to it like this, it was another manifestation of her fundamental indifference to the welfare of her children that they remembered from their childhood. Well, indifference cut both ways. The past was irretrievable and one could not develop an affection for someone in old age.

In fact, now they came to think of it, she has been partially responsible for their divorces, if not entirely so. Despite her indifference to her children, she has summoned up enough interest in them to despise or disparage their choice of wife. She would label their wives NQOCD before they were married, *Not Quite Our Class, Dear.* Her lip would curl slightly, in a way perceptible only to her sons, who sensed that her low opinion was as much of them as of their proposed spouses.

Moreover, she made her daughters-in-law subtly aware of her disapproval, that she thought no person of quality would consort with them. She made them feel awkward, underbred, unwelcome, intrusive and inferior. Thus she had vitiated her sons' private lives, for no better reason than a love of interference and exertion of power for its own sake. Now they came to think of it, she had never been very likeable; she was fortunate that they had found Edentrees for her, which was more than she deserved.

Roger and Felix decided to come into their inheritance before their mother's death, which surely could not be long now. They did so by borrowing on expectations as collateral, from banks and from friends. True, Felix's reputation among his friends for repayment of loans was patchy at best, but he had never mentioned his expectations so explicitly before, in terms of such proximate fulfilment. Moreover, he could exert a charm such that his unreliability seemed almost a virtue; his friends tended to be rich and thought they were doing humanity a service by keeping Felix afloat. They certainly never regarded him as the type of cad who intended to make off with the money. As for the banks, they required proof only of Mrs Marsh's age and that she possessed capital: they did not concern themselves what Felix (or Roger) wanted a loan for.

Though Mrs Marsh clung limpet-like to life, yet she grew ever frailer. Her refusal to eat became more insistent and she began to lose weight, a bad (or a good) sign. She wanted to lie all day on her bed and grew angry when interfered with in any way. Her outbursts of rage against the staff became more frequent: she would strike out at them with her stick. This became so intolerable that Dr Elliott had to be called. There was nothing for it but to sedate her. He ordered pills at first, but she would sweep away with her hand the little plastic cup in which they were offered her, or spit them out petulantly if they were placed in her mouth. The staff asked Dr Elliott for permission to give her injections, and he agreed, provided only that they thought they were in personal danger from her aggression. This, of course, they soon learned to do.

One day, Mrs Marsh threw a cup of tea over one of the nursing assistants, a young Polish woman who delivered meals to the residents. Fortunately, it wasn't very hot, but she claimed that it had scalded her. It was not the first time that Mrs Marsh had lashed out at her, and now she was frightened of her.

'She is become very dangerous lady,' she said to the Matron.

The Matron knew she had to act. People like this nursing assistant – conscientious, reliable, hardworking – were not easy to find, and were become ever more so.

'I'll give her an injection,' said the Matron.

Soon afterwards, a strange wailing was heard throughout the wing that emerged from Mrs Marsh's room, followed by an eerie silence. Mrs Marsh had struggled a little, but she was no match for the Matron and the two nurses she had taken with her.

The injection kept her quiet: a little too quiet. She lay back on her bed, her mouth agape. She was almost impossible to get out of bed, but the difficulty was not her normal resistance to doing whatever she was asked. She was generally floppy but stiff in her limbs, and moaned rather than complained. The Matron ordered that she be propped up on pillows but kept sliding down the bed and lying flat, however many times she was propped up again.

'The injection'll wear off,' said Matron.

The next day, however, Mrs Marsh appeared to be gasping, taking in weak little breaths. Her mouth opened and shut like that of a goldfish in a bowl.

'We'd better call Dr Elliott,' said the Matron.

Dr Elliott pronounced the end near.

'The old man's friend,' he said. 'Bronchopneumonia. Or in this case, the old woman's.'

He decided against treating Mrs Marsh.

'Thou must not kill but needst not strive officiously to keep alive,' he said sententiously.

'Shouldn't we ask the relatives whether they want her treated?' asked the Matron.

'Their wishes have no legal standing,' said the doctor. 'It is up to us to act in Mrs Marsh's best interests when she lacks capacity to decide for herself. Besides,' he added, lowering his tone as if disclosing a secret, 'in my experience, more relatives of people like Mrs Marsh want them dead.'

The Matron called Felix: he was the one to call in case of emergency.

'I am afraid I have some rather bad news for you,' she said, Felix's heart missing a beat for joy. How he had longed for this bad news! 'Your mother has pneumonia. The doctor says she hasn't long to live.'

'When... when?' said Felix. Not a bad imitation of distress, he thought.

'It could be any time now,' said the Matron. 'She probably won't last the night.'

'I'll come straight away,' said Felix. It was most inconvenient, but Mrs Marsh was wearing a large and valuable diamond ring. He wouldn't have wanted one of the others to get hold of it. He would have to cry off Michael Smyth's dinner now: he had been thinking of touching him for a few thou.

By the time Felix reached Edentrees, Mrs March had passed away peacefully, as the Matron put it. For form's sake, Felix went to see her, but he was thinking of the next move, at least the move after he had informed his brothers. He would phone Mummy's lawyer first thing tomorrow morning. But what time was first thing for a lawyer, he wondered as he left the bedroom with Mummy's corpse still on the bed. Nine? Half past nine? Ten?

He settled on ten. It would not do to look too eager. Mr Rotterson, the lawyer, said it would be best if all the brothers came to his office at the same time. Felix asked him when was the soonest he could see them, and promised to convoke his brothers.

The three brothers duly arrived at Mr Rotterson's office. They did their best to look grave. They shook hands with Mr Rotterson by turns, and he asked them to take a seat.

'You've come, I suppose, about the will of your late mother.' It was not really a question.

The three brothers inclined their heads slightly, as if there were other, more important things on their minds.

Mr Rotterson, whose movements were slow and deliberate, drew a long, narrow brown envelope with heavy black writing on it towards him across his desk. With long fastidious fingers, he drew a document from it, and unfolded it.

'This is the last will and testament of your mother, Mrs Adelaide Marsh,' he said. He paused for a moment. 'Do you want me to read it all, or just her instructions as to the disposal of her estate?'

The brothers looked at one another. Each was reluctant to speak his preference.

'Just the disposal,' said Felix, the most courageous, after a pause.

'I'd better read a little bit more,' said Mr Rotterson, 'just to explain things.' He slowly donned his half-moon reading spectacles framed in tortoiseshell.

'My three sons, Roger, Felix and David, having so neglected me during the last twenty years of my life, and having proved themselves throughout their lives unable or unwilling to perform any useful work, I give and bequeath all my worldly wealth to the Frimley Donkey Sanctuary, Registered Charity Number six seven nine three five two.'

Mr Rotterson removed his spectacles from his nose, folded them and placed them carefully on his desk.

'Naturally,' he said, 'I tried to dissuade your mother both from the wording and the actual provisions of her will. Unfortunately she was determined and I did not succeed.'

The three brothers were silent for a moment. They were shocked. Who was their mother to accuse them of having done no useful work? Talk about the pot calling the kettle black! She had never done a stroke of useful work in her life. All she had ever done, ever since her childhood, was amuse herself and order other people about. She hardly knew what washing up was like, let alone working for a living. It was preposterous, hypocritical, unjust!

But that was not really the point. The will was terrible and had to be overturned.

'When was the will drawn up?' asked Felix.

Mr Rotterson put on his spectacles again and looked at the bottom of the envelope.

'A little less than four years ago,' he said.

'Mummy wouldn't have known what she was doing then,' said Felix. 'She wouldn't have known her own mind.'

Mr Rotterson bridled a little.

'I drew up the will myself,' he said. 'I assure you that if I had had the slightest doubts about your mother's mental capacity, I should not have done so.'

And indeed, Mr Rotterson seemed to exude probity like a secretion.

'Did you have her examined by a doctor before you drew up the will?' asked Felix.

'I did not think it was necessary,' said Mr Rotterson. 'I had no reason to do so. She was perfectly lucid.'

'But she was over ninety,' said Roger.

'It's not a question of age,' said Mr Rotterson firmly. 'It is a question of capacity, and that I assure you your mother had.'

'Didn't you think that the very absurdity of the will was evidence that she didn't know what she was doing?' asked Felix.

'It is not for me to interfere with the last wishes of my client or to pass judgment on them. I am his or her agent, not his or her master.'

'Well, we'll see about that,' said David, gritting his poet's teeth. He stood up to go. Felix and Roger stood up too.

'We want to protect our mother's reputation,' said Felix. 'She would be a laughing stock among her friends if they ever got to hear that she'd made such a will.'

'She must have made earlier wills,' said David.

'I assure you that this will is valid. As executor, it is my duty to ensure that its provisions are carried out as nearly as possible.'

The three brothers repaired to the nearest café. Roger would have preferred a bar, but it was not easy to find one at that time. Cafés were alien to him, and made him feel uneasy and out of place, like a polar bear in a jungle.

'There are three grounds on which we can challenge the will,' said Felix. He had done a little research beforehand. 'The first is that Mummy was not competent to make it at the time she made it, and the second is that she was under undue influence when she made it.'

'Rotterson seemed pretty shifty to me,' said Roger. 'All that probity act. I wouldn't trust him further than I could throw him.'

'Don't be ridiculous, Roger,' said Felix. 'He's been Mummy's lawyer for years. And your suspicions aren't evidence.'

'Lawyers stick together,' said David lugubriously.

It was true. One of Roger's wives had been a lawyer and she had defended her partner even when he ran off with the clients' money. She had also received very favourable treatment during the divorce.

'The other ground on which we could challenge the will is that it fails unreasonably to provide for dependents who are in need of the money, and that she had promised it to us.'

'Well, we all need money, that's for sure,' said Roger.

'But do we count as dependents?' asked David.

'The courts are flexible,' said Felix, 'but in both directions. You never know with them. The judge might take the view that we are a lot of wasters who deserve nothing.'

'Maybe you two,' said David. 'At least I write.'

'We must be more deserving than a set of bloody donkeys,' said Roger.

'The best approach,' said Felix, who, relatively speaking, was an authority, 'would be to find a previous will when there was no question of her capacity.'

'Mummy was always making wills,' said Roger.

'Threatening to cut us out,' said David.

'Depending on which of us had annoyed her most recently' said Roger.

'It's a risk we have to take,' said Felix. 'Otherwise the donkeys get it all.'

'I never knew Mummy liked donkeys so much,' said David.

'She didn't, like donkeys.' said Felix. 'She hated us.'

'What if we find that one of us is cut out of the will before?' asked Roger.

Felix had considered this.

'I think we should agree that, come what may, we should all be equal beneficiaries, whatever the will says.'

'And what about all the money you borrowed from Mummy and haven't paid back?' asked Roger.

'We can deal with that later,' said Felix.

They agreed to split the estate three ways, irrespective of whether one of them (impossible to predict which) had been cut out of the previous will – which was still hypothetical.

'Good,' said Felix. 'Now we'll need a lawyer of our own.'

'Why?' asked David.

'More money down the drain,' said Roger.

'We'll have to force Rotterson to divulge previous wills. Obviously, he won't do so of his own free will.'

So they went to see Mr Grabbage, a friend of a friend of Felix. He was very reassuring.

'I'll write to Rotterson,' he said. 'He'll have to divulge previous wills.'

But Rotterson proved more obstructive than anticipated. He demanded good evidence that there were any grounds for doubting the validity of Mrs Marsh's last will before she died. Was there any such evidence?

'Rotterson's just being awkward,' said Mr Grabbage. 'Playing silly buggers. I'll write to him again.'

The second letter, however, was no more effective than the first.

'I'm afraid Rotterson's closed up like a clam,' said Mr Grabbage the next time the brothers came to see him. 'We'll have to force him to disgorge what we want.'

'How?' asked Roger with suspicion in his voice. The two lawyers were dancing a *pas de deux* at their expense, and that of the estate.

'We shall first have to demonstrate that your late mother lacked capacity at the time she made her last will,' said Mr Grabbage.

'How?' asked Roger again.

'Well,' said Mr Grabbage, 'I shall of course take statements from all three of you as to your mother's condition at the time. But that will not stand us in very good stead, because you're interested parties and in any case Rotterson would argue that memory is variable and capacity comes and goes, it isn't just fixed, yes or no. We'll need more than that.'

'Then why bother?' asked Roger. He was thinking of the costs, that were mounting vertiginously, like a sheer wall that rock climbers like to tackle.

'It would look very strange if we didn't,' said Mr Grabbage. 'It would look as if we had something to hide and didn't really believe in our own case. It would be the first thing a judge would ask: why are there not statements from any of the sons?'

'So what next?' asked Felix.

'After I have taken your statements,' said Mr Grabbage, 'I shall have to instruct a medical expert, preferably two or three.'

'To do what?' asked Roger, almost angrily. 'To charge a huge fee? Mummy's dead, isn't she? We have her death certificate. We didn't kill her.'

'Nobody is saying or even suspecting that you did,' said Mr Grabbage. 'The medical expert will look at your statements, but he will also examine your late mother's medical records to assess whether, in his opinion, your mother did have capacity.'

'And what if he decides that she did?' asked David.

'We find another expert. You can find one to say anything.'

'And if he says the same?'

'In my experience, it doesn't take long to find one. Most experts say what their instructing lawyers want them to say: not, of course, that we tell them what we want them to say. But they guess anyway.'

'And then?' asked Roger.

'The problem is that the same is true of the other side. It will find its experts to say what it wants them to say.'

'So they cancel each other out?' said Roger.

'Not exactly. The judge then has to decide which expert evidence he prefers. That's what we have courts and barristers for.'

'So it boils down to a question of which is the better expert?' said Roger, his pitch rising.

'I wouldn't say better,' said Mr Grabbage. 'More convincing or plausible, perhaps. But it isn't only the expert evidence that counts.'

'What else?' asked Roger.

'The evidence as a whole,' said Mr Grabbage. 'The preponderance of the evidence.'

'I suppose experts are expensive?' asked Felix.

'I'm afraid so, especially in a case like this, in which there is no fee laid down and where there is a large estate. But it all rather depends.'

'On what?' asked Roger.

'On what the judge's decision is. The loser might have to pay all the costs.'

'If we won, they would come out of the estate?' asked David.

'Well, yes,' said Mr Grabbage, 'but at least you wouldn't have to pay them yourselves.'

'So we lose whatever happens,' said Roger.

'I suppose you could say that,' said Mr Grabbage. 'But you really don't have any choice if you want to inherit anything at all.'

The brothers saw this at once, but didn't want Mr Grabbage to think that they would agree automatically to anything he said. They didn't want to be putty in his hands or his milch-cow either.

'We'll think about it,' said Felix, as they left his office.

The time, out of consideration for Roger and because of the hour of day, they repaired to a pub, but their meeting was short because there was nothing to discuss.

'We'll have to do what he suggests,' said Felix. 'Otherwise it's everything to the donkeys.'

'What if the previous will...? asked David vaguely.

'No point in speculating,' said Felix briskly. 'We'll have to take the risk. Anyway, it could hardly be worse.'

The process was slow. The experts retained by both sides were busy men who could not consider the case for several weeks, if not months. Besides, the first report (for the brothers) was unsatisfactory: the expert found no evidence of incapacity. Mr Grabbage was not in the least put out by this, and lost none of his equanimity. It was simply a question of finding another expert, he said, though this of course entailed more expense and delay. He suggested a modest down-payment of £25,000 to cover costs so far, which, he said, was very reasonable in the context of the expectations.

The money was not easy for the three brothers to raise, however, because they were nearly at the end of their credit; but somehow, they managed.

The second report, six months later, was much more favourable to their case, but it was cancelled out by the report for the other side.

'I'm afraid,' said Mr Grabbage, 'that brings us back to square one, just as I suspected it would. We shall have to seek counsel's advice.'

Counsel charged £7,500 a day, but again there was no choice. They had to continue, or Rotterson would claim his own costs on behalf of donkeys, whose interests he was obliged, as executor, to defend.

'What happens next?' asked Felix.

'The experts meet and prepare a joint statement,' said Mr Grabbage. 'That is to say, they state what they agree and disagree about. Unfortunately, it sometimes takes them weeks or months to prepare the statement. I'll apply to the court to set a date.'

The application, of course, was not free of charge; and when finally the joint statement arrived, it simply reiterated the opinions of the two experts in the first place.

'What now?' asked Felix.

'Old Rotterson is being very obstinate: he hasn't shifted position at all. I looks like we'll have to go to court. However, the case won't take long: a day or two at most: that's the good news.'

'And the bad?' asked Roger.

'The bad is that the court costs are £50,000 per day minimum. Of course, they're recoverable if we win.'

'From our own estate,' growled Roger.

'And if we lose?' asked David.

Mr Grabbage remained silent for a moment, as if in memory of fallen soldiers.

'If we lose, you have to pay them,' he said.

Felix noted that 'we' became 'you' whenever it was a question of money.

'And what are our chances?' asked Felix.

'Our chances? I would put them above fifty-fifty. Perhaps sixty-forty.'

'What happens if we win?' asked David.

'Well, of course, that's just the beginning. I can't possible say what's in the former will, if there is one. Only Rotterson knows that.'

A few days later, Felix received a call from Mr Grabbage.

'Rotterson's made an offer,' he said.

'What is it?'

'I think I ought to tell you all in person,' said Mr Grabbage.

His office had now become familiar to the brothers. In this case, familiarity bred dislike.

'Rotterson's unexpectedly caved in,' said Mr Grabbage, 'Or almost. He's offered to release the old will to us – without prejudice, of course.'

'What does that mean?' asked Roger mistrustfully.

'It means that he releases it without admission of its validity. He still holds the later will to be valid. And there's another condition,' added Mr Grabbage, as if it took the shine off the good news.

'And what's that?' asked Felix.

'That each side agrees to bear its own costs.'

'It's outrageous!' exploded Roger.

'I agree,' said Mr Grabbage smoothly. 'But what are our alternatives? We could go to court, of course, in which case we might win and you would have no costs. But we might lose, and then... There is always the alternative of dropping the whole matter.'

The three brothers were left in a state of rage too deep for words. They could have strangled the world. That old villain Rotterson, with his air of half-adviser, half-retainer, had made a packet already from the estate. The brothers wouldn't have been surprised to learn that he'd been plotting it for years. Eventually, Felix regained control of his tongue.

'I suppose we have no choice,' he said. Old gambler though he was, he would not accept odds of sixty-forty, even if they were given disinterestedly.

'There is always a choice,' said Mr Grabbage sententiously.

'We're no further on,' said Roger. 'We're back to where we started.'

'There's no need to say the obvious,' said Felix with asperity.

'But no further back,' said Mr Grabbage brightly, as if that were a silver lining.

The three brothers gathered again for the reading of the previous will.

Mrs Marsh, being of sound mind, and disgusted that neither Felix nor David had visited her for the previous three months, did give and bequeath her entire estate to her darling son Roger, who had at least visited her once during that period.

'The old bat!' exclaimed David involuntarily.

'I told you that you ought to visit her more often,' said Roger, who had said no such thing.

'It can't be valid either,' said Felix. 'When did she make it?'

It was dated six months before the last will.

'There you are, you see!' said Felix. 'She was just as bad then as she was later.'

'On that argument,' said Roger, 'she could never have had capacity.'

'What do you mean by that?' asked Felix angrily.

'Four and a half years ago, wasn't that just after Mummy's ninetieth birthday?'

'What of it?'

'Which you didn't attend.'

'And so?'

'I remember that Mummy was perfectly well then. And everyone else at the party said it was amazing how good she was. She knew what she was doing.'

'Don't be ridiculous,' said David. 'How could she have known what she was doing when six months later…?'

'And how could you know that she didn't? You weren't there.'

'It was more likely that you didn't know what you were doing,' said Felix. 'There was plenty of booze there. You might as well try to keep a pig from a trough.'

'We agreed that whatever the will contained, we would share equally,' said David.

'I think we should obey Mummy's wishes out of respect for her,' said Roger.

Felix let out a little laugh of derision, like a small, sputtering firework.

'I suppose you'll use the money to raise a monument to her,' he said.

Mr Grabbage, who had watched the dispute with professional detachment, asked them what they wanted him to do, how to proceed.

'Do nothing,' said David. 'Nothing until we have considered our position.'

'On the contrary,' said Roger. 'I want you to try to have this will proved.'

'There seems to be some division between you,' said Mr Grabbage.

'I want you to continue to act for me,' said Roger.

'But not for us,' said David and Felix, almost in unison.

The brothers divided on leaving Mr Grabbage's office: Roger going off in one direction, and David and Felix in another.

'Roger's a snake,' said David.

'Always was,' said Felix. 'Do you remember…?'

They began to reminisce about incidents from childhood in which Roger had kept toys for himself that he wouldn't share.

The two brothers decided that they needed a lawyer of their

own to contest the validity of the two wills and search for a third, yet older, in which Mrs Marsh had left everything to the brothers at least equally. If she had cut Roger out, so much the better. Besides, natural justice must count for something, even under English law.

'I'd rather the donkeys had it than Roger,' said David.

'At least it'd do some good,' said Felix. 'They'd use it more intelligently. Roger'd just piss it away.'

A lawyer, Mr Franklin, told them that they could challenge the will on three grounds, incapacity, undue influence or inherent unreasonableness: in which case, there might be a previous, better will.

Shortly afterwards, however, Roger began to exhibit gratifying signs of illness consequent upon his long-term habit.

'Let's hope it's nothing trivial,' said Felix.

'No one could say he's led a healthy life,' said David.

It was cancer, and quick-growing too. No one had asked for it more, said Felix. His flesh melted away, as did his appetite; he even turned down drink. It all happened in weeks. The hospice beckoned.

Roger died. More importantly, he died intestate. Felix and David returned to Mr Grabbage. As Roger's legatees by default, as they supposed, they wanted him to act for him. Mr Grabbage agreed: there were no hard feelings between them.

A few weeks later, he called Felix and David to his office.

'I'm afraid,' he said, 'there's been a bit of a complication.'

'What?' asked the brothers anxiously.

'The two ex-wives have come out of the woodwork. 'Actually, only one of them is ex. Her divorce didn't quite go through. Anyway, they must have heard of your late brother's demise. They're claiming a share of his estate – in fact, all of it.'

'Vamps, they both were,' said David.

'Are,' corrected Felix. 'What do we do?'

'There are two possibilities,' said Mr Grabbage, 'not mutually incompatible, or at least employable in succession. We can contest the validity of the will leaving everything to Roger, and find another, prior will, or we can claim that the financial settlement of his wives was full and final, and that therefore they cannot be his legatees.'

'Would it work?' asked David.

'It might. The problem is that, whatever the law says, judges are often sympathetic to ex-wives.'

David and Felix left Mr Grabbage's office both depressed and angry.

Women!

Nasal Congestion

I T WAS HIS NOSE, his nose alone that prevented his happiness.

It was not as if the young man asked much of life, after all. Indeed, he hardly knew what the word ambition meant. If asked what he wanted to do or be, he might have replied 'I wouldn't mind being a baker.' But since his nose had taken on its grotesque shape, even that modest aim was quite out of the question. He could leave his little maisonette in William Wordsworth Way only under cover of darkness, or under compulsion of need, for example for cigarettes. Who but a circus clown would expose such a nose to the mockery of the multitude?

While his nose remained as it was, he could not hope for a companion. When he looked in the glass, all he saw was his nose. The rest of his face was regular, even quite good-looking in a commonplace way: but his nose ruined everything and drew attention to itself like a lighthouse on a dark night. He examined it several hours a day, from every possible angle; it was getting worse, defying description. He tried draping a towel over the bathroom mirror but it was no good: that was merely shooting the messenger. He could think of nothing but his nose, and once he had draped the towel over the mirror he could not resist the impulse to lift it and take another look to see whether it had changed.

If he went out, people laughed at him, or sniggered. He heard anything from a short explosive 'Ha!' to a hearty 'Ha! Ha! Ha!' Sometimes the laughter came from the other side of the street or from an open window, in which case it was indistinct. Passers-by whispered about him, too, always about his nose of course. Didn't they have anything to talk about but his nose? He didn't hear exactly what they said, but it was obvious what they were saying. They stared at him as well, but when he caught their eye they looked away guiltily. They didn't do that to people with one leg or missing finger: why did they do it to him, then? Of course, one's nose was more important than a leg or a finger.

Now he went out only with a scarf wrapped round his head, from his chin to just below his eyes. People shied away from him, pretending to imagine that he was a robber: but really they knew it was his nose that he was covering up in this fashion. Its fame had spread, the whole city knew about it.

From time to time his mother would telephone him.

'It's got worse,' he said, without having been asked.

His mother didn't understand; she was exasperated. She had no sympathy; anyone would have thought that she wasn't his mother.

'Not your nose again.' She would say. 'Why can't you just forget it? There's nothing wrong with it.'

'You're only saying that to shut me up,' he would reply. 'You can see it as well as me.'

Why did she persist in her pretence? It gave him no relief, quite the contrary. Probably she felt guilty at having given birth to such a monster. If only she would tell him the truth, then they could have a proper conversation. Instead, she tried to distract him with things in which, with a nose like his, he couldn't possibly be interested: his Aunt May had died, John next door had had an operation for his hernia, there was a fresh leak in the bathroom. There was always an edge in her voice, as if she knew that she was only talking for the sake of it. Her calls were an embarrassment to them both.

Sometimes, when he was particularly insistent about his nose (what a bore, as well as a worry!) she would lose her tem-

per. One day she said to him, 'Why don't you go to the bloody
doctor, then, he can give you a new nose!'

Strangely enough, he hadn't thought of that before, but of
course it was right, they could do anything these days: turn men
into women and women into men, a new nose was nothing by
comparison. With a new nose, his troubles were over.

He didn't like to go to the doctor for the same reason that
he didn't like to go anywhere else. He would have to sit in the
waiting room with everyone staring at him, or at least wanting
to do so. But this time he went with a sense of purpose, almost
of optimism. He would have to remove his scarf, of course, and
show the doctor his nose, which would be humiliating, but the
doctor would understand at once what needed to be done, send
him straight to a surgeon, and then his new life would begin.
His Calvary would soon be over.

The doctor called him into his consulting room. He had not
yet removed his scarf.

'What can I do for you?' the doctor asked, pleasantly
enough, though a little puzzled by the scarf.

'It's my nose,' the young man said, his voice muffled.

'Broken?' asked the doctor. Pub fights were not uncommon
in the area, and neither were broken noses.

'Look!' said the young man, removing his scarf with a de-
spairing flourish.

The doctor looked, even peered, at it. He could discern
nothing out of the ordinary. It was not obviously broken, nor
did the patient sound as if he were breathing through any internal obstacle in it which would have to be removed.

'What are your symptoms?' he asked.

Symptoms? What a question! Was it not obvious that his
nose was the affliction, the malady, the burden, the handicap,
the deformity, the cross to bear? Was the doctor a fool, or merely being falsely polite, or mocking him, stringing him along,
playing with him as a cat with a mouse? He had expected him,
when he removed his scarf, to recoil in horror or even disgust at
what he saw. But he had done no such thing: he had exerted an
almost inhuman degree of self-control. Or maybe he was nearly

blind.

'Can't you see it?' he asked.

'See what?' replied the doctor.

'My nose. It's deformed, disgusting. Everyone else can see it. They look at me, laugh at me, whisper about it.'

Although the doctor now knew that it would do no good, he tried to be reasonable.

'Your nose is perfectly normal,' he said. 'You're a good-looking young chap. You should go out and enjoy yourself.'

Enjoy himself! Would he have said that to a hunchback or a leper, go out and enjoy yourself? What was the difference between him and a hunchback or a leper?

'Look!' he said, growing agitated, and pointing with shaking finger to his nose.

'What's wrong with it?' said the doctor. 'Describe it to me.'

Oddly enough, considering that he had thought of nothing else for the past year or so, he found it difficult – no, impossible – to put into words. After a pause, he said:

'It's like a monster growing on my face, yes, a monster, eating it away.'

Again the doctor peered at it.

'It seems all right to me,' he said, knowing that what he said was futile, even stupid.

His patient was now desperate. He jabbed his finger in the direction of his nose.

'Look, look!' he said. 'It's spreading like a fungus! It's growing! It's a cancer! It's all red and raw! And the bone is sticking out!'

The young man was obviously not going to be persuaded otherwise. He needed treatment, some pills.

The doctor tapped something on his computer.

'I'll write you a prescription,' he said.

'A prescription!' the young man repeated with disgust. 'That's not what I need, a prescription's no use to me. There's nothing wrong with me, I need a new nose, that's all.'

'I'm not saying there's nothing wrong with your nose,' said the doctor, trying a little sophistry where plain reason would not work. 'But it's the way you see it, you've got it a little out of proportion.'

'You're telling me it's not my nose, I'm mad, that's it, isn't it?' He got up to go. 'I'm not mad. It's my nose. You're just saying it's all right to save money. If it was your nose, you'd have it operated on straight away. I want a second opinion.' He ran from the room in a state of rage and despair, and slammed the door after him.

Once home, his thoughts about his nose, which had hitherto enjoyed a monopoly in his mind, were admixed with hatred of the doctor. He would have to see his partner, a woman doctor. Women understood these things better, they were not blind or ruthless like men.

Once he had convinced the receptionist that he wanted to see the woman doctor, he returned to the surgery. He explained to her what was wrong. She was very sympathetic.

'Yes,' she said, in a motherly way. 'It must be terrible.'

'I want to see a surgeon,' he said. 'Who can give me a new nose.'

She could tell that he would be satisfied with nothing less, and she did not want to be reproached with having stood in his way. It was the only way he would leave the room satisfied, and perhaps he would accept a surgeon's word, you never knew. Human beings were unpredictable: one minute they were mad and the next they were sane. And vice versa, of course.

'There's a waiting list to see him,' she said.

'I don't mind,' he said, calming down. 'I've been waiting long enough already.'

He returned home almost cheerful (although still concealing his nose). There was light at the end of the tunnel and a new, better life stretched out before him: a girlfriend, parties, the cinema, a job, holidays. Surely it was only what he – everyone – had a right to? He was asking only for what everyone else had.

The wait was long. A letter arrived to tell him that it would be six to nine months. This was unfair, but he realised that there was nothing he could do about it: he was powerless and that was the way the world was. They didn't care, they didn't understand, but they would cure him in the end. The time passed slowly, but eventually the appointment arrived.

The hospital was dingy, but the surgeon transcended it. He flowed upwards from the floor in a tall, elegant arc. He had obviously been born a success. Doubt, and all the troubles that doubt brought with it, were unknown to him. There was no need for arrogance: politeness was enough, and was as natural to him as song to a blackbird.

He listened to the young man before him (he had heard it all before), examined his nose carefully, held a ruler to it, felt it with a light touch. The young man awaited his verdict like a man awaiting the verdict on a capital charge.

'I think we can help you,' said the surgeon. The young man's heart leapt for joy. 'But before I can operate, I'll have to send you to a colleague of mine.'

'What for?' asked the young man, somewhat deflated.

'I have to have his permission,' replied the surgeon, knowing that it would never be given, but transferring the opprobrium of refusal to someone else. 'He has to ensure that the operation will do you more good than harm.'

The young man was puzzled. How could a change of nose do him anything but good? Of course, all operations could go wrong, but the young man knew that they rarely did these days.

'What do you mean?' he asked the surgeon.

'Unfortunately,' said the surgeon, used to the question, 'resources for this kind of surgery are limited. The government insists that we operate only on the most pressing cases.'

The young man was taken aback. It had never occurred to him that there were cases other than his own, let alone that someone might consider them more important than his. No one, after all, had ever had a nose such as his; no one had ever seen anything like it. His case was unique.

'He'll ask you a few questions, that's all,' said the surgeon.

The surgeon shook the young man's hand and patted him on the back.

'After I have his report,' said the surgeon, 'I'll send you another appointment.'

The young man returned home in a state of ecstasy quickly alternating with despair. Yes, he would have his operation and the new life beckoned; but no, it would not be immediate as he had hoped, and might be long or indefinitely delayed. There might even be treachery afoot.

And the wait indeed proved long, especially as the days and minutes were dragged out by hope and expectation. Surely a message would come soon? They could not leave him dangling, like a man at the end of a rope.

The weeks and months passed: two, three, four. Still no appointment, no appointment from the surgeon's colleague whose approval for the surgeon to operate. The young man went to the hospital – his face wrapped as usual – and approached the counter marked Appointments. The woman behind the counter was shuffling some papers into a pile and did not notice him until he cleared his voice through his scarf.

'Yes?' she said, looking up at him.

'They said they would send me an appointment,' he said.

'Who said?' she asked.

'The surgeon.'

A faint smile played over the woman's face.

'Do you know how many surgeons we have here?'

'The one that's going to do my nose.'

'A plastic surgeon?'

'I think so.'

'We have four. And each of them has two deputies.'

'He's very tall.'

'Do you want me to hold an identity parade?' She was pleased with her little sally. It broke up the monotony.

'He talks posh.'

'That's hardly surprising. Most of them do. You don't expect them to talk like...' She paused to think of a suitable likeness. 'Like dustmen.'

'Anyway, he said this other man would send me an appointment to ask me some questions.'

'We don't make appointments here,' she said. 'We only check the appointments people already have, to make sure they've come at the right time on the right day.'

'Where do I get my appointment, then?'

'You have to wait, like everyone else. If they said they'll send one, they will.'

The young man retreated. He didn't want to expose himself to the public for too long, even with his scarf round his face.

The appointment did eventually come, however, both by e-mail and post. He returned to the hospital.

The man whom he now saw was a very different type from the surgeon. He introduced himself by his first name, Gary, and told the young man that he could call him Gaz because everyone else did. His sparse grey hair was drawn back into a kind of ponytail, or at least a tuft. He was the hospital psychologist.

The young man was irritated, puzzled and fearful. What had psychology to do with his nose? You couldn't make it small or straight or normal by thinking about it. A nose was something physical, not mental.

'I don't know why I'm here,' the young man said.

'It's routine procedure,' said Gaz. Despite his bohemian appearance, Gaz was a stickler for routine. 'All clients wanting elective plastic surgery go through it.'

The tests began. The young man still couldn't see the point of them. First he had to move some wooden bricks around, like he had at play-school. Then he had to make a few sentences up that contained three words that Gaz gave him. Finally, he had to fill in a questionnaire, ticking whether he agreed or not, and how strongly, with statements about himself, such as 'I feel nervous around other people.'

It all took an hour and a half, after which Gaz thanked him.

'What happens now?' the young man asked.

'I write to the surgeon, and then he sends you an appointment.'

'What about my operation?'

'That depends on the surgeon.'

The young man waited, he had no choice. He thought of suicide, the various ways he could do it. There was car exhaust, but he didn't have a car. He could jump off a tall building, but the thought of the impact on the ground put him off. He could jump out, or lie down in front, of a train, but he knew that he would change his mind at the last minute. He could hang himself, but what if he didn't do it properly? The very thought of cutting his wrists immediately gave him an uncomfortable feeling in his wrists. He knew he would scratch them rather than cut them. As to poison, he didn't know which to use. No, he would give it a little more time and then decide.

Again, though, an appointment came, this time for the surgeon. It was now several months since he had first seen him, but a tidal wave of hope surged through him. The new life was approaching.

It was not the surgeon who greeted him, but his deputy: a younger version of himself in the making.

'I have discussed the case with the boss,' he said. 'And I'm sorry to have to tell you that our colleague has decided that you would not be suitable for an operation. He thought it would do you no good. He said that any operation you had would not satisfy you and you would want another immediately afterwards.'

'So when will my operation be?' asked the young man, who appeared not to have heard.

The deputy's irritation was only internal, his superior had taught him never to show it.

'I'm sorry to have to tell you that we will not be able to operate on you,' he said. 'The decision is out of our hands.'

The young man understood at last.

'You mean I've got to go on like this!' he cried, in the tone of a wounded animal. 'How would you like it if it was you?'

'I'm very sorry,' said the surgeon's deputy. 'But resources are limited and we have to shepherd them as best we can.'

The young man had a flash of inspiration, desperation having stimulated his mind.

'What if I went private?'

The surgeon's deputy was careful not to exhibit a change in attitude.

'That might just be possible,' he said. 'But I have to warn you that it would be very expensive.'

It was obvious that the young man had no money, but in cases such as this people with no money often found it one way or another, in a way that they never would for something more worthwhile.

'How much?' asked the young man.

'It's impossible to give you an exact figure,' said the surgeon's deputy. 'It'd be up to the boss.'

'Roughly?'

'Well, I think about ten thousand pounds, if it all goes without any complications. Not that I would envisage any in your case.'

The young man's thoughts were now racing. The question of how to raise the money drove everything else from his mind. He was almost happy.

'The boss would want you to think very carefully before you went for it,' the deputy surgeon said. 'Whether it's really what you want.'

His conscience clear on the matter of having duly warned him, the deputy surgeon said he would ask the boss to take the young man on as a private patient. He gave the young man the boss's card, to phone for an appointment at the private clinic when he had made his decision (he knew that the decision was already made).

'But I must warn you,' he said, 'that the clinic would require payment in advance. The clinic insists on it, and we have to obey its rules.'

This was only partly true: only some patients had to pay in advance, those who were uninsured or could not really afford it.

The young man went away satisfied. It might not have been fair – why should he have to pay for what others had free? – but this was a small thing by comparison with the relief that beckoned. Ten thousand was a lot of money, but it was not an insuperable problem to find it. His mother had more than that in her savings. In fact, she had at least thirteen thousand.

He went to her. He did not get on very well with her, but he know that she had a guilty conscience towards him. He had never known his father, who had decamped either just before or just after he was born, even his mother did not quite remember anymore. He had had a variety of stepfathers, with only one of whom had he had any relations of affection. Charlie had taken him to the park and even to a football match or two, but his mother had shown Charlie the door after a few months without any explanation, and never allowed him back. Her other boy-friends sometimes lasted a little longer, if they behaved badly enough, and they either ignored him or made their distaste for him plain enough (he was evidence of her antecedent infidelity). Now that he had grown up, she realised that she had not provided him with a good home or upbringing: in fact, she was lucky that he had not gone to the bad, as had so many of the other boys around her brought up in the same way. If it wasn't for his absurd obsession with his nose, all might have turned out unexpectedly well. But she knew, or believed, that peculiar obsession must have had something to do with the way she had brought him up.

When he came to her, he explained all that the surgeon and his deputy had said. He could have the operation if he paid for it; and he knew that it would change his life.

His mother offered only token resistance, feebly objecting once or twice that there was nothing wrong with his nose, that he was a good-looking boy as he was, that his nose was quite in keeping with the rest of his face. But she had tried such arguments many times before and knew that they did not work, so she gave in, and agreed to give him the majority of her life savings, inherited four years before from her own mother's death.

She drew the money from her bank in cash.

He took it, two hundred notes, to the private clinic where the surgeon operated. The person in the office was used to this manner of proceeding: it was how all people who could not afford their operations paid for them. The surgeon would see him very soon.

The appointment came three days later. The clinic was very different from the hospital. Your feet sank into the carpet and there was silence rather than continual clatter. No one seemed rushed, yet everything was done quickly. He was immediately offered tea or coffee and asked what kind he would like. He was offered a biscuit with a thick chocolate coating. He still wore his scarf, but if they noticed, they were better at concealing it. Indeed, they spoke to him as if he were some kind of boss himself.

The surgeon called him into his office. It was a splendid room with a great mahogany desk and heavily-lined silk curtains. The surgeon rose with outstretched hand to greet him.

'Good morning,' he said. 'How nice to see you again. How are you?'

'I'm all right, but I've come about my operation.'

'Yes, of course,' said the surgeon, as if his memory had been jolted. 'Quite so. The first thing we have to decide is what kind of operation to perform.'

'It's on my nose.'

'Yes, but we have to decide what kind of nose you would like. You have a choice.'

Strangely enough, the young man had not considered this, not for a moment that he had been preoccupied by his nose and its deformity. So disfiguring was it, so incompatible with normal life, that he had supposed that any nose other than the one he possessed would lead straight to happiness. The precise details of alternative nose had been of no concern to him. Indeed, on the occasions that he walked in the street, as few as possible, other people were for him characterised principally by their beautiful, normal noses, whatever their size and shape. He envied and resented them: why should he alone of all the people in the world be afflicted thus?

The surgeon handed him a kind of brochure with close up photos of various noses, all of them incomparably superior to his.

'I cannot absolutely guarantee to reproduce exactly any of these,' he said, 'but usually I can manage a fair approximation. Of course, it depends partly on what I find at operation.'

The young man looked at the noses as a glutton looks at a box of chocolates. It was difficult to choose, all looked so good, every single one a passport to happiness.

'Perhaps I could help you with some advice,' said the surgeon. He looked at the young man appraisingly, like a portrait-ist stepping back from his canvas to look again at his subject. 'Some would be easier than others, less likely to result in complications.'

'Complications?' said the young man.

'Well, as you know,' said the surgeon, 'not every operation is completely successful, even if the great majority are. Quite apart from the very small risks of any operation whatsoever, anaesthetic accident for example, which is almost unknown these days, and there is the faint possibility that the operation will not work and a second might be necessary to correct it.'

'You mean…?' The young man did not know what the surgeon meant.

'Plastic surgery is not carpentry and flesh and bone are not wood,' he said. 'We work with living tissue which sometimes has a will of its own. It may do something unforeseen, not that I anticipate anything like that in your case, but I have to tell you, it is required of me. But I am confident that your operation will be straightforward, though we'll have to wait two weeks afterwards before the final result is evident.'

'So I will have a new nose?'

'Oh yes, that I can absolutely guarantee.'

The young man returned to looking at the photos. He preferred something slightly aquiline, but not too pronounced, rather than something retroussé.

'Here,' he said, pointing to the photo: a nose that no girl would be able to resist.

The surgeon looked at it.

'Yes,' he said, 'I think that should be possible.'

The operation was fixed for a week's time: but a week is a long time to wait for salvation. Times slowed almost to immobility, but not quite. The day eventually came and the young man returned to the clinic. Before the operation, another doctor gave him a form to sign, which he neither read nor understood, even after the doctor had explained it. He wasn't listening.

The operation was a success, that is to say without immediate complication. When he came round from the anaesthetic, the young man's first thought was to look at himself in the glass. He told a solicitous nurse that that was what he wanted, but she told him that his nose has a large dressing over it and he would be able to see nothing. He should rest.

He was sent home the next day with strict instructions not to remove the dressing on pain of ruining the surgeon's delicate work. He should return in a week and in the meantime take it easy, indulge in no strenuous activity. He should not be alarmed at the appearance of puffiness or black eyes: they would resolve.

He looked at himself repeated, as if the last time he might have been mistaken as to what he had seen. Human flesh was not clay that took on any shape desired without protest, as it were.

He was constantly torn between obeying instructions and taking a look at what was beneath the dressing. The latter, unfortunately, had been applied in such a way as to be impossible to look beneath without destroying it, or at least severely damaging it. With immense self-control akin to torture, he left it in place.

The day came for its removal. When the nurse had finished, the surgeon entered.

'Good morning,' he said, jovially polite on this, the most important day of the young man's life so far.

The young man, who had never been taught the refinements of politeness, replied, 'All right?'

To the inexperienced, his appearance was somewhat alarming. Both his eyes were blackened, as if he had been the loser in a fight. (In his area, to have been in one fight invited being taken on in another.) Worse still, his nose was swollen and therefore misshapen, and now genuinely disfigured.

'Perfectly satisfactory,' said the surgeon with the air of a connoisseur. 'It'll take a few weeks to settle down, then you'll see.'

The young man looked in the glass above the washbasin, and let out a cry of horror.

'It's horrible!' he exclaimed. 'Worse than before.'

The surgeon repeated his reassurance that all would be well in a few weeks' time. The black eyes would disappear, the swelling subside, and the true new nose would make itself evident.

'I promise you,' said the surgeon. 'You'll have the nose you wanted.' In the meantime, he should avoid sneezing, blowing his nose or anything like that.

Once more the young man was condemned to wait. He was suspicious of the surgeon's assurance that all would be right in the end. He spent hours in front of the bathroom mirror, but a watched swelling never goes down. Then gradually his bruises turned rainbow colours and faded, and the swelling did subside. By the time he went to see the surgeon again, neither bruising nor swelling was visible.

But that did not mean the operation had been a success, far from it. His nose was worse than ever. How could he face the world with such a nose? The surgeon had deceived him. He had told him it would be better and now it was far worse. The money he had taken to do this was the least of it. He had left him crippled, grotesque, a monster, a freak! Everyone would stare at him more than ever – or laugh at him. The surgeon must put it right, that was the least he could do!

'Look at what you've done!' exclaimed the young man, distress and rage struggling for the upper hand.

'Let me examine you,' said the surgeon calmly. He had faced these situations before.

He revolved his head around the young man's nose, looking at it from every angle.

'There is,' he pronounced, 'a tiny deviation to the left, so slight that it is invisible to the untrained eye.'

Tiny deviation, is that what he called a gargantuan excrescence! It was all very well for him to talk, but he did not have to live with such a nose! He had no feeling, no conscience, no shame. But he would have to put it right, he would have to!

'What are you going to do about it?' asked the young man with a hint of menace in his voice.

The surgeon put his hand to his chin as if in deep thought. After a pause, he said:

'I would leave it well alone. As I said…'

Leave it well alone! Leave him like this for the rest of his life!

'You've got to do something,' the young man screamed so that the people outside the room could almost hear. The tone at least would have reached them. 'You can't leave me like this! It's you what done it!'

The scene was turning ugly, and the young man was on the verge of losing control of himself. Goodness knows what he would do then.

'Calm yourself,' said the surgeon, making patting gestures in the air with his hands. 'Lower your voice. We can perhaps do something…'

'What?' asked the young man, like a tiger pouncing.

'It would take another small operation to correct it.'

The young man's rage subsided, though his pulse still raced. 'When?' he asked.

'We" have to wait a few more weeks for it to settle down completely, for full healing to take place. It wouldn't be wise to do it straight away.' The surgeon looked at a calendar on his desk. 'Here,' he said, pointing to a date, 'would that suit?'

The young man nodded.

'There is only one thing,' said the surgeon. 'I will, of course, perform the operation at no cost, no charge.' He was fully aware of his own generosity, of his own adherence to professional ethics. 'And I'll speak to the anaesthetist. I think I can persuade him to waive his fees. But I cannot do anything about the clinic charges, they are out of my hands.'

The surgeon pushed back his chair back, the beginning of the end of the consultation.

'How much will it cost?' asked the young man.

'Five thousand pounds, give or take a hundred or two.'

Five thousand pounds! It was impossible. He knew no one with that kind of money and couldn't ask his mother again, even if she had had it. The thought of robbing a bank crossed his mind, but that was ridiculous. He didn't know how or where he could get a gun. You needed experience to rob a bank, and anyway it was wrong.

What about shoplifting? That was much less wrong. When he was younger, he had taken a few chocolate bars from Mr

Patel's newsagent without having been caught (but had Mr Patel really not known?). To raise five thousand pounds by shoplifting was different, though. How would he sell what he stole? He knew that people bought stolen goods at only a fraction of their price in the shops. He would have to steal an enormous amount, therefore, and the likelihood is that he would be caught. It was completely impractical.

Five thousand pounds! The sum revolved in his mind without any accompanying thought as to how to raise it. Five thousand pounds! The words were like an insect that burrowed into his brain. Then, suddenly, a solution, or at least an explanation, came into his mind.

The surgeon had known all along that he would never be able to find five thousand pounds and therefore never intended to operate and put his nose right. Not only had he maimed him, but he had made a fool of him. Furthermore he had known from the first than an operation would ruin his life. The surgeon was not only a bungler but a criminal.

But why him, why had the surgeon selected him for his fraudulent attentions? His mind went back to the clinic waiting room. There had been plenty of normal people sitting in it, all with normal noses. The meaning of this was now clear to him. Why hadn't he thought of it before? The clinic had been an elaborate charade to ensnare him, and he, like a fool, had fallen for it. The more he thought about it, the more obvious it was, the more certain he became. It was additionally humiliating that he had not seen something so perfectly plain before his very eyes. God, how the surgeon must be laughing at him!

Well, he would have his revenge: but how, that was the question? They thought they could treat him any way they liked just because of where he lived, because he didn't know who his father was (his mother had always dismissed his enquiries by saying, 'Oh, you don't want to know'), and above all because of how he looked. He would teach them different.

But what form would it take, his revenge? A slogan painted on the clinic wall – something like, *We steal your money and make you worse* – might cause them a moment's discomfort, but it would soon wear off, and anyway they would paint over it. No, it had to be something else: they had to be stopped, these thieves, these swindlers, these MURDERERS! And now he realised that what they had done to him, they must have done to others. He had not realised it before because they hid themselves away from sight in the same way that he did. By avenging himself he would be avenging others, doing a good deed. It would be a lesson to the whole country.

The idea of taking action buoyed him. He almost forgot his nose, or at least pushed it to the back of his mind. First things first! After he had dealt with the clinic, then he could solve the problem with his nose.

But still the problem of method remained. He could burn the clinic down, and the image of a can of petrol came to his mind's eye. But it would have to be at night, and he would have to break in. The clinic would surely have been alarmed, and he had no experience of breaking into premises, unlike some of the young men around him. And then the fire might not take: it might only make a bit of a mess.

It was the surgeon who was behind it all, who was the evil genius of the whole rotten scheme. Without him, it would collapse. Without him, there would be no clinic. The solution was obvious: he must be eliminated.

He attended his clinics on Wednesdays, that much the young man had discovered. But since he had attended only to be cured, as he had so stupidly thought, he had failed to take any real notice of the grounds in which the hospital stood, where the surgeon parked his car, where he could conceal himself, and so forth. He therefore reconnoitred the grounds and discovered that there were some thick bushes by the car park reserved for the medical staff. There was a gap in them, too, convenient for leaping out from: at long last, he was in luck.

The following Wednesday, his heart beating wildly, he concealed himself behind the bushes. He watched the doctors arrive in their expensive cars. They did not suspect that they were being watched. As they got out of their cars, they all consulted their telephones for messages to reply to. This, too, was fortunate, for it slowed them down and made the easier targets. Someone who was moving fast would be harder to strike.

The surgeon arrived. His car was the best, the most expensive, of all of them. This proved that he was indeed in charge of the whole sham organisation, just as the young man thought.

He leapt out from behind the bushes, having drawn his long and sharpened kitchen knife. Having raised it high, he plunges it between the surgeon's shoulders, just as was gathering his things from the back seat. The knife met with more resistance than the young man had anticipated, but the surgeon swivelled round and he was able to plunge it upwards into his belly. The surgeon uttered a strange cry, between a scream and a gasp, as he fell. Blood seeped quickly though his clothes.

The young man suddenly felt his arms gripped from behind. Someone shouted 'What are you doing?' though it was obvious what he was doing. Several people rushed at him and wrestled him to the ground, where he felt slaps around the head. What happened next was a blur in his memory, snatches of scenes in unfamiliar rooms, men in informs, questions being asked of him, a sandwich and tea in a chipped mug.

When he came to, he was in a strange residence where people kept giving you orders. People who called themselves nurses gave you pills which they said you must take. The other people around you shuffled, gesticulated and spoke gibberish. What was he doing there? They were nothing like him. The only problem with him was his nose. Their noses were normal.

DOMINATION

ALFRED SMITH HAD dedicated his life (or so it might have seemed to an observer) to proving that character is destiny. He had every gift a man could have for success in life, other than character. It was his character that was his downfall.

He was the son of a factory worker who had had the misfortune to be born when a man of his high intelligence could receive scarcely any education beyond what he could later obtain for himself during his few hours of leisure, and had been put out to work as soon as he was able. He was determined that one of his four children should receive the education that he had not had, and Alfred, being the one who early showed the most aptitude for studies, was the one chosen. At great sacrifice – for times were hard and wages were low – he encouraged, demanded that, Alfred stay at school long after he might have gone to work and thereby contributed to the household economy. At first all went well, for Alfred was a capable pupil who absorbed knowledge quickly and had the knack of passing exams with ease. He was fortunate in his teachers, dedicated men who did everything in their power to open the world of learning to their best pupils and encouraging them on a path that would lead them out of the slums. Not that they were purely utilitarian: they believed in mental cultivation as a good in itself. They recognised Alfred's ability and nurtured it.

At the age of fifteen, however, Alfred began to form a conceit of himself and his superior abilities that was compounded by a native sensitivity to slights of any kind that he began to perceive where none was intended. As his teachers opened his eyes to the world beyond the slums, and to occupations of the mind other than horses, football and pub brawls, he developed a disdain for that world into which he was born without developing a love for the world beyond it. He looked down on everything from the heights of his intelligence, including on his father whose sacrifices had made an escape possible for him. His father, though intelligent, was not articulate and spoke the language of the slums, which Alfred quickly apprehended was no asset in a hierarchical world. He set about learning to speak as his teachers spoke, and was so successful that it soon became second nature to him to do so. He was determined that no one should ever guess his origins by the way he spoke.

At the same time, Alfred was painfully aware, and could never forget, those origins. In a twisted way, he was even loyal to them, not because he loved them – far from that – but precisely because he detested them but was unable to forget them. It was as if he had been born with a deformity that no surgery could cure. When a person spoke to a hunchback, he might make every effort to conceal that he was constantly aware that he was speaking to a hunchback, but the hunchback himself could never shake off the suspicion that he was being condescended to.

For the rest of his life, then, Alfred was fully at his ease with no one. He feared and disliked those born of higher social status than himself while he felt disdain and even contempt for those born of his own lowly status who had failed to rise. His life was long and uncomfortable.

He won a scholarship to university – something rare and precious in those days – but failed to take it up. His father, normally a placid man, was furious and did not speak to him again for two decades, until just before he died. He did not forgive his son his headstrong decision which he could not understand, and which made a mockery of his, and the rest of the family's, sacrifice. He did not see that there was fear in his son's arrogance.

At the age of sixteen, Alfred had been infected by politics: not just by any politics, but by the kind of politics, Marxist, which gave him and others like him a complete understanding of the world, or so they thought. Why go to university when you understood everything already, especially as, at university, they would try to indoctrinate you with false ideas? Everything from the workings of nature to the machinations of capitalism was now clear to Alfred; and far from having to learn anything from the world, Alfred had everything to teach it. From these heights he would never afterwards descend, whatever setbacks in life he experienced.

He brought the good news of the inevitable coming of the new world without want, without classes, without conflict, of complete quality, to his family, but they, with the blindness of people who could not see beyond their noses, did not believe it: they lacked the education to understand it. Even as he depended on his family for his daily bread, he felt contemptuous of them.

Alfred began to spend his time at dismal meetings in cold and draughty halls, spreading word of the inevitable. At first he was inseparable from his mentor, George, an ill-favoured youth a year or two his senior, who had inducted him into the mysteries of the doctrine, but with whom he subsequently broke over some minor aspect of orthodoxy. The fact is that Alfred could not make friends for long with anyone: for true friendship, whose art he was never to master, was impossible without some kind of equality, and Alfred could no more tolerate equality in practice than he could deny it in theory. The only relations he could endure for long were those of master to disciple, with him the master; but disciples were difficult to find, and even more difficult to keep.

Alfred took early to smoking a pipe, as some grow beards to be, or to be taken as being, venerable and wise. He thought it gave him that gravitas which otherwise young men are inclined to lack. Besides, the greatest man in the world smoked a pipe (it was possible for Alfred to admire him without reservation, to the point of worship, because he was an abstraction rather than a being of flesh and blood who might sit across the table from him), and therefore pipe-smoking might confer greatness. What began as an affectation soon became a deeply-ingrained habit; and throughout the rest of his life he left a trail of ash and acrid smoke behind him which he thought a small price for anyone to pay for his company, and even as part of his charm.

While caught up in the world of dingy meetings and the distribution of tracts to the downtrodden, who seemed ungrateful for the favour, Alfred discovered also the expensive pleasures of life such as women and restaurants. He saw no contradiction between his political views and the good life: after all, the object was to bring the good life to within the reach of all. Sometimes it was necessary to seize the day.

Not bad looking and possessed of physical vigour, Alfred found it easy to attract women, though somewhat harder to retain their interest: not physically, but mentally, for before long he treated them, too, as disciples, and they did not much care for it. He was attracted particularly to women of higher social class than himself, though he did not disdain to use women of the lowest social class for fleeting sexual pleasure. The problem with those of higher social class, however, was that he had always something to hide from them, and this he could do only by the assumption of intellectual superiority. Alas, though highly intelligent, he remained an autodidact with many lacunae in his knowledge and experience, which sooner or later became obvious: and this was made worse by his early assumption of complete understanding, which obscured from him the necessity to learn. Among his faults were impatience and an intolerance of the tedium necessary to achieve the mastery of anything; and he lacked the humility to acknowledge the superiority of those who possessed those qualities. Patience he equated with slowness of mind.

He therefore had always to appear what he was not, a kind of panjandrum or renaissance man. He could impress at first, for he had indeed a quick mind, supplied with a patina of the latest knowledge; but before long his dogmatism about every subject upon which he spoke – and he spoke on many – would also reveal his ignorance. He would lay down the law which he derived from his own first principles (which, of course, were not truly his own) on subjects to which he had never previously given a moment's serious thought; and then he would tolerate no opinion other than his own. Other opinions provoked him to bluster, and if persisted in, to anger. Thereafter, no person of spirit could endure his company.

He felt more at ease, then, with people of lesser, and even much lesser, intelligence than his own, though at the same time they could not satisfy him or gain his respect. He knew in his heart, and even in his mind, that it was no achievement to impress or to dominate those lacking in intelligence; and so he was inexorably drawn to those who were bound before long to reject him.

He had another more pressing and practical problem: how to earn his living. Not only had his father withdrawn all monetary support from him because of his failure to take up the scholarship, but in any case he had not the means to support the kind of life that he desired. Alfred therefore came up against the brute fact that, though he understood the world so well in general, he was not immediately able to shape it to his liking. For the moment, he would have to accept it, and make his way in it, as it was at present constituted. In short, he had to look for work.

He had two disadvantages in this search. First he lacked any particular qualification or skills, and second he could not tolerate a position of subordination, being told what to do. His intelligence being far greater than that of those who gave him orders, he could only quarrel with them and tell them it should be done better. Moreover, he did not want to be the source of someone else's profit, an endless source of surplus value. He preferred to mount his own business, and if that meant the exploitation of others, it was only because present-day social conditions forced it upon him. When the time came, as inevitably it would, he would cease his participation in the iniquitous system.

But what business? As a young man with a totally scientific

outlook (he would have studied science at the university had he studied anything at all), he knew that science was the future. It was, so to speak, the infrastructure of the future, of the life to come; all else was but superstructure that was bound to decline in importance. It was the tangible that would count, not the froth, such as advertising and entertainment, of a degenerate capitalist society. And of course, science could not be carried out without scientific instruments: that much was clear from his schooling.

He also knew that he lived in a wasteful society: in fact, it was a society built, in effect, on waste, for without it there would be no demand and the system would collapse. Therefore some people threw out as surplus what others desperately needed: there was surely some profitable way to connect the two. Had not his teachers at school complained that they lacked the proper instruments to teach science as they would have liked, while schools for the rich discarded more equipment than schools for the poor had ever had?

It occurred to him, then, that he might buy discarded or surplus instruments from rich schools and sell them at a profit – the devil drives where needs must – to the poor. If he made a profit, it would at least have been in pursuit of a useful social end. By helping to have instilled a scientific outlook in the minds of the children of the poor, he would at least have brought forward their inevitable eventual liberation from capitalism.

But even starting in a very small way required a little capital. This he borrowed from one of his brothers, less educated than he, who had been sent out to work at the age of fourteen and had become a butcher on his own account. He was an ardent gambler on the horses and dogs, and was either flush with money or broke. Alfred touched him for money when he was flush, and like many gamblers he was generous when in funds. Though he paid him back, Alfred was soon to forget what he owed him in a larger sense: after all, he would eventually have found elsewhere the money to start, all that happens in the world being inevitable.

Alfred's scheme worked in a small way, and gradually in a

larger one. It might have done so quicker if he had not wanted, or needed, so urgently to impress women of a higher social class for the short duration of their liaisons (the outlay for such liaisons being greatest at their commencement). Before long, he employed an assistant but strangely enough, though he sympathised with the impoverished and subordinate in general, he found the individual instances of these large groups who worked for him profoundly unsatisfactory, lacking in intelligence and initiative, and common sense as he defined it: namely, doing things in precisely the same way and order as he would do them himself. The timid lasted longer with him than the spirited.

Alfred lost his temper easily when something went wrong, and so enjoyed his tempers that they went wrong constantly. He felt no remorse afterwards, rather a sense of freshness or relief after a storm. He was always right, and his exposure of the deficiencies of others – their idiocies, in fact – increased his confidence in his own judgment. If anyone had told him that his bullying of staff was unnecessary and even inefficient, let alone morally wrong, he would have said that he lost his temper only for educational purposes: people had to learn. But even if he had been convinced that there was more money to be made by mansuetude than by harshness, he would have chosen the latter. He preferred to be more feared than loved.

All the same, his business prospered. He began to deal in new instruments as well as old, and finally only in new. He needed an office and then a secretary. He chose secretaries not for their secretarial ability, but by their appearance, social class and potential for seduction. He set about the latter, combining it with humiliation, for example by finding fault with their grammar to impress them with himself. They seldom stayed longer than a few months and he always said that he was glad to see the back of them.

Then the war came. He was exempted from service because his business, though small, was deemed to be of national importance or utility. This was a relief, not only because he had no vocation for the profession of arms and felt none of the attractions of danger, but because, had he been obliged to fight, it would have been against the then-ally of the Hope of Mankind. And in fact, his business flourished during the war, relatively-speaking, for scientific instruments were more than ever necessary, though he did not become rich as a result because his train of life became more expensive.

He married for the first time during the war, a pretty young woman of good family that had fallen on hard times but that did not see Alfred as a suitable match. She had been his secretary. Samantha and he married early in their affair, as falling bombs and the uncertainty of survival led many people to do; they did not really know each other, and in particular Samantha did not know Alfred. She soon learned things about him that caused her to repent at leisure, just as her family had predicted that she would.

Principal among his faults was Alfred's satisfaction at nothing and dissatisfaction with everything. He would taste the food she put before him as if he were deciding a difficult point of law, and then, after a suitable delay during which her tension mounted, pronounce upon it, or rather upon what was wrong with it. There was too much salt or not enough, never precisely the right amount. The slightest of her activities was subjected to the same microscopic examination and criticism: and it was as if everything she did were of world significance. He did not tell her in advance, however, how anything should be done, so that there should be no chance of her complying exactly with his wishes and thereby destroying grounds for complaint. It was obvious that he did not care for anything much in itself, except as an opportunity for criticism.

When he pronounced on the difficult and delicate question of whether an egg had been boiled too long or not long enough, but never just right, he did so like a learned man or as Euclid proving a theorem from whose conclusion there was no derogation. His likes and dislikes were matters of fact, not of taste or judgment; just as there was only one law of gravity, there was only one length of time an egg should be boiled to achieve the right consistency.

It was not in his nature ever to bestow unstinted praise. If, as was unusual, he uttered some words of praise, for example that there were no spelling errors in a typed letter, he would at once qualify it by pointing out that, on the other hand, the margins were too wide or too narrow. He lived in a world (of his own making) in which there was a fixed quantity of praise that could be bestowed: and the more for others, the less there could be for him.

Alfred did not want his wife to work: it would be a sign of his failure if she did so. This meant, of course, that he needed another secretary and he set about not only finding one, but seducing her. The first two whom he employed did not stay long: they quickly found his political opinions, uttered with papal authority, together with his fault-finding, intolerable. The last straw was when he asked, or expected, them to attend one of his dismal political meetings in draughty hall to celebrate the glorious efforts of the former enemy-turned-ally; they preferred dancing. His politics were for his attractiveness to them what nausea is to appetite.

A third was made of sterner stuff: she excited his ardour by proving more difficult to seduce. She was pretty, and of a family of a distant county which she had come to London to escape. Alfred found himself, for the first time, constrained to control his impulse to criticise and denigrate: it would obviously do him no good with her to give it rein. He was surprised at how easy it was, but nevertheless resented the necessity. For once he was patient: there would be time enough later for his revenge. She was alone, after all, and vulnerable.

He did not tell her at first that he was married, certainly not until the wall had been breached. In those days, adultery, however widely practised, still had the connotation of sin, and divorce was spoken of, if at all, in hushed tones. But once the first step had been taken, it was far easier to tell her because the point of no return had been reached.

He concocted a story – a far from original one – to explain his infidelity, naturally placing the blame on his wife. He conferred upon her every fault from an unwillingness to understand him to frigidity of every kind. He was, in fact, her victim: she had not revealed herself to him before the marriage, which she had entered too eagerly, too hastily. In fact, she had entrapped him; and now he was paying the price for it.

He explained his absences from home to his wife by pressure of work and business trips, which were long and arduous during wartime. At the same time, however, he did not mind if she discovered the truth, in fact he quite wished that she would. Not only would it make it easier for him to continue, but it would put her in her place. Besides, it hardly increases respect for a woman that she believes the lies that she is told. He therefore left theatre tickets around for her to find.

'Why,' asked his wife, as he had expected her to do, 'were you late last night?'

'I was working,' he said. 'There's a big order and it's not going to be easy to find a way of filling it.'

'Especially in the middle of the night,' said Samantha.

'It's not just a question of talking to people on the phone, you know.'

'No, you have to take them out to the theatre as well.'

'What do you mean?' Alfred asked, though he knew very well.

Samantha showed him the tickets she had found.

'I take staff from time to time,' said Alfred. 'You ought to know that. It's good for their morale.'

It was a lie that he did not even intend that she should believe and Alfred was not altogether displeased to see the pain on Samantha's face. A woman in pain was likely to be submissive.

After a week or two of unusual attentiveness to Samantha, Alfred returned to his previous conduct. He claimed pressure of work to explain his late arrival home; Samantha did not believe him and he had not supposed that she would. He did not even disguise the occasional impress of lipstick on his face: his carelessness was calculated. Her family had never liked him and were likely to take the view that she had made her bed and should now lie on it.

The war over, Alfred had established himself in a small but secure way. He often gave people whom he met for the first time the impression that he was a scientist of some description, but when pressed admitted that he was 'in' scientific instrumentation rather than in science proper. Being in sounded better than merely dealing in. Alfred now felt his absence of formal education as a wound, a wound that would never heal, but best dressed or plastered over by bluff. He retained his faith, however, in his fundamental understanding of everything.

Shortly after the peace, Samantha fell ill. She tired easily, bruised easily and before long could scarcely rise from her bed. A blood test proved that she had leukaemia and in six weeks she was dead. Alfred buried her without much regret and never looked back to visit her grave. He was not a sentimental man.

During Samantha's last illness he had continued his affair with Felicity, who was soon to be his second wife. In fact, Samantha's death had been rather timely, in so far as it had obviated the need for and expense of a divorce. By now, Felicity was fully enamoured, and failed to reflect fully on his conduct; she listened uncritically (though also without positive assent) to his materialist lecture that death, after all, was only the natural end of life and therefore nothing to concern oneself unduly with. The state of non-being was not to be feared or mourned in others. It was nothing more special than eating and drinking. One must be rational.

There was no question, therefore, of a decent interval. But to his surprise, and not altogether to his pleasure, he began to feel more for Felicity than he had for any of the others. He even had some kind of affection and respect for her, which troubled him. He did not altogether like the feeling, for it presaged a limitation of his freedom. To betray with no conscience was one thing, to betray with a bad conscience another.

At first, though for a very short time, they were happy. He restrained himself and it was only when she was pregnant for the first time that he was unfaithful to her. He persuaded himself that it was because she was ill and tired all the time during her pregnancy that he sought consolation elsewhere. And after the baby was born, a boy, she was depressed; and though he liked the baby well enough, after ten minutes with him he was bored. There had been millions of babies born in the world and, speaking rationally, there was no reason why his should be special just because it was his.

Felicity discovered his infidelities, and resolved to return as his secretary. That way, she could keep an eye on him and his activities. They had enough money to employ a nanny, a middle-aged German woman fleeing the conditions of post-war Germany. Felicity, sensing another danger, selected her for her unattractiveness.

Alfred resented being spied upon at work, as he conceived it. That he had done something to deserve it did not moderate his feelings of irritation, if anything the reverse, for there is no resentment like that of the justly-accused. She caught him one day in the act of fondling the nanny, Fraulein Blick, notwithstanding her unattractiveness. In this instance, it was not so much a betrayal and an insult.

Fraulein Blick was henceforth not to live in, but consigned to a room above a nearby shop. It would not have been easy for Felicity to separate from Alfred, first because she had a young child, but second, more importantly, she had a passion for Alfred which she expressed by a certain coldness towards him. This was an excellent way of retaining Alfred's interest in her which, however, could not be exclusive. It nevertheless maintained his respect for her, rather as a mountaineer respects a rock-face. Alfred's pride was piqued; he could not fully betray Felicity until he had overcome her resistance to him. And so there grew between them a relation of hostile dependence, with neither yielding entirely to the other.

A second child was born to them. As the child grew, Alfred veered between indulgence and severity towards his offspring, with a preponderance of the latter, and between pride in them and irritation. As they grew, they became more of an encumbrance to him, and he either ignored or lost his temper with them, not because they ever did anything very terrible, but simply because they had not fully complied with some trifling order of his or other. He did not care what they did, so long as it was what he had told them to do.

There was silence now at home between Alfred and Felicity. He had long since ceased to lecture her on every subject under the sun as if she were a potential disciple whom it was his duty to educate. She had even sometimes demonstrated that she knew more of the subject he was talking of than he. This might have been humiliating for him but for his power to disguise it from himself, thus preserving his awareness of being always in the right. Once, when she was acting as his secretary, he said that she had spelled a word wrongly and ought to change it. She insisted that she had spelled it correctly.

'Get the dictionary,' he ordered.

The dictionary proved that Felicity had been right.

'Get another dictionary!' ordered Alfred.

Did he mean it? He did. He insisted that his was a recognised variant spelling of the word, and a further, fuller dictionary would prove it. He sent Felicity out to the nearest bookshop to buy the largest, most comprehensive and authoritative dictionary in stock. It too proved that she had been right all along, and that there was no alternative spelling. Alfred then discoursed on how language changed, how common but illiterate usage eventually became correct, and how in his childhood (he was ten years older than Felicity) the spelling he had suggested had been the correct one. All the same, he never corrected her spelling again, signing her letters exactly as she had typed them. This, too, he resented.

His business grew and he converted into shares the money that his brother had lent him to start it. Alfred never forgave his reasons to be grateful to his brother, so much less intelligent and educated than he, and he took his revenge. His brother had fallen on hard times and needed a job. He gave him one as a packer, working in the basement as if he were the madwoman in a Victorian novel, never allowing him to come upstairs to meet the customers or business associates, in case he should give away Alfred's origins; but he paid him exactly what he paid himself. In such a way did Alfred humiliate him for years on end. He knew that he would never forego the excellent pay for the sake of his dignity; and he knew that his brother knew that he knew it. Humiliation was much more gratifying than exploitation.

In fact, Alfred was much more interested in the domination of a small group of people, provided that it was absolute, than in becoming rich. His habit of fault-finding was not, as it is with others, the expression of perfectionism or fastidiousness, but of the urge to feel large by making others feel small. The smaller they were, the larger he was. He lost his temper and threw whatever came to hand at the wall. He did not care a fig for whatever it was that he lost his temper over: that was not the point. It was to make himself feared. Naturally, his staff did not stay long, and would not have stayed as long as they did had he not been generous with money, to which – for a businessman – he was strangely indifferent. He did, however, have one loyal servitor who stayed for many years: he was extremely hard of hearing.

Alfred's insistence on oversight and criticism of the smallest details of what his underlings did meant that the business could not grow beyond a certain point, for even his abilities were limited by time. When his competitors outstripped him in size, it was because, in his opinion, they had adopted the wrong methods and principles that were bound in the end to lead to disaster. Thus Alfred was a success if you measured him from where he started, but a failure by comparison with what he might have become. If he knew it, he never admitted it, not to others and only equivocally to himself.

Felicity gave up work and retreated into a glacial silence, extending also to the children. There was a silence in the household when both Alfred and Felicity were present that was more than the mere absence of sound: it had an almost positive quality. Visitors sensed it at once; it made them uncomfortable, anxious to leave and not to return. Felicity could not disguise her bitterness from her children: it spilled over into her care of them. This care she confined completely to their physical needs, to which she attended with an almost compulsive exactitude, against which the children later rebelled. She would not allow them to meet her own family as if she ashamed of them, being incontrovertible evidence of her physical liaison with her boorish husband whom they had never liked and against whom they had warned her.

If his children were present, Alfred imposed his will on them; if they were absent, he gave them no thought. All the same, he insisted on their choice of career without reference to their wishes or inclinations, but simply on the basis of some principle or opinion that he plucked from the air but which, once he had plucked it, became law to him. They went their own way as soon as they were able, and once (very quickly) he had got over his anger with them for having disobeyed him, he forgot about them. They would be neither a burden nor a comfort to him.

Unknown to him, Felicity has resolved to leave him as soon as the children had left definitively. Her departure was a blow to his *amour propre*, but not otherwise a cause for deep mourning. At the time, he was conducting another affair with a secretary called Bridget.

He was now in late middle age. He had long noticed that secretaries these days, thanks no doubt to the liberation of women, who now had a wider choice of career, were of markedly lower social class than they had once been. This had its conveniences, for it made it cheaper, if less satisfying, to seduce them and excite their admiration. Bridget appeared much in awe of Alfred.

Until Felicity left him, Alfred had not thought much about his own future: it stretched indefinitely before him as an endless continuation of his present existence, whatever it was at the moment. He now realised that his possibilities and choices were fewer. He had no wife, his children had escaped (or fled) him, his brother would not talk to him; and he had no friends because he had no gift for friendship. But he also had no vocation for solitude.

About this time, a competitor offered to buy his company. It was for a comparatively large sum that Alfred thought would be sufficient to last him the rest of his days. He might not have another such offer and he knew that there would come a time when he would tire of, or be unable any longer to do, the work. He accepted the offer.

He took Bridget to a restaurant, the most luxurious she had

ever seen, and broke the news to her. His plan was to buy a place in the country and live there quietly. He had always been a keen gardener, and gardening was what he proposed to do. He would be self-sufficient in vegetables. In the midst of his explanation, he had time to taste the wine as if he were an oenophile (which he was not), and discuss his findings with the sommelier, who was obliged to listen to him. He also sent something back because it was over- or insufficiently cooked. To be completely satisfied with nothing was his way of proving his worldliness and sophistication to Bridget, who observed it with admiration.

Then, almost abruptly, he asked Bridget to come and live with him, to share his life with him. She was surprised, or at least affected surprise. She was in her forties, already dyed her hair, and was rather commonplace, neither pretty nor bad-looking. Her worst feature was a slight squint, but no so bad that you were unsure whether she was looking at you or at something else. She had recently separated from her own husband, a drunken waster. Her only daughter, Lisa, was grown up and had married young. She spoke with a slight nasal whine and had not much to say for herself, which did not displease Alfred. He had always had enough to say for two.

Bridget said that she would have to think about it, but they both knew that it was for form's sake, that she would accept. What were her prospects if she did not? Now that, for the first time in his life, Alfred would have to spend whole days, weeks and months in the company of a woman, he would need one who was completely dependent on him. Bridget filled the bill – nothing and nobody was perfect in Alfred's eyes – at least adequately.

Alfred looked for a house in the country and soon found one. He did not think it necessary to consult Bridget on the matter, as he was the one who was paying for it after all. He thought it best to begin as he intended to continue.

They moved in together. Bridget showed herself appropriately delighted, pleased (at first) with everything. Neither of them had ever lived in the country before, but you would never have guessed it from Alfred's discourse on the quality and properties of the soil, the climatic conditions, the insect pests, the necessity of earthworms, the proper placement of clothes lines, the direction of the wind in relation to flourishing or otherwise of fruit trees, and so forth. Bridget listened, apparently willing to learn, though close observation of the intermittent nods of her head might have revealed that they were at random. She retained little of what she was told.

As a cook she did not come up to Alfred's mark. Even a boiled egg was beneath her capacity to get right, and Alfred had to show her how it was done correctly. Then he would take the egg that he had boiled himself, taste it and declare it to be just right, as if no egg had ever been so satisfactorily boiled before.

They had joined the ranks of the middle classes, but Alfred, at least in theory and for the purpose of exposition, remained true to his ideals. In the countryside of rolling hills, lawns and well-tended fields, he would lecture Bridget on the coming grand expropriation, though for the moment he seemed content not to be expropriated.

'What'll happen to us?' asked Bridget one day, after one of his disquisitions.

This was a question so stupid and typically petty bourgeois that Alfred would have been angry had it not provided him with another opportunity to put her down as mentally inferior.

'I'm not talking about us,' he said. 'I'm talking about the movement of history in accordance with its laws. You are like a dinosaur that asked 'What will happen to us?' before the asteroid landed that wiped them out.' Alfred, who had watched a television programme about the mass extinction sixty-five millions years ago after a massive asteroid collided with the earth, was pleased with the analogy. He had always had a gift for exposition and might have been a teacher if it had not been a waste of his talents. 'Why must you always brings things down to a personal level?' he asked.

Bridget, who had no regrets at having escaped her previous impoverishment (Alfred was not mean with money and seemed to care little for it) shrugged off his prediction of well-merited extermination as if she could fully grasp neither the inevitability nor the magnitude of it.

'I suppose you must be right,' she said.

Of course he was right. Had he not been studying the question for years, while she had not given it a moment's thought even had she been capable of it? Then he resumed his gardening, which had become the true passion of his life. Plants never answered back.

The garden flourished under his care. He had green fingers and might have been a professional. The only problem was that the garden was large – more than four acres – and he began to have difficulty in kneeling and bending. Late middle age was sliding, perceptibly, into early old age. He complained of this to Bridget.

'We're none of us getting any younger,' she said with her usual talent for saying the obvious and uninteresting.

Alfred's doctor was hardly any better. He said that arthritis was only to be expected at Alfred's age. For once, Alfred was on the receiving end of a homily. Studies had shown, he said, that, after a certain age, arthritis was inevitable to some extent (greater or lesser as the case might be), and that, apart from analgesics, whose continued use he did not advise, there was nothing to be done short of replacement of the hips and knees, which was not yet necessary or justified.

Alfred was incensed by the doctor's useless generalisations about everyone of his age. He was an individual, not a member of a herd. The doctor mistook his duty. How could you trust someone like that, who spoke in clichés, even if everything he said were factually correct?

The arthritis grew worse, just as the doctor said it would, and just as Alfred had always known that it would: he had not needed the doctor to tell him that. The mornings were particularly difficult, and he was not one to suffer in silence. He informed Bridget of his condition as if issuing a bulletin on the health of a head of state. Bridget received the information with gradually increasing indifference, which she hardly tried to conceal. Her commiseration, when she uttered any, was abrupt or abstract, as if with someone she knew only by hearsay. He thought that it should have been more heartfelt, considering all that he had done for her. Sometimes she merely repeated what the doctor had said, that at his age it was only to be expected.

'Since when have you had a medical degree?' asked Alfred irascibly.

'You don't have to be a doctor to know that,' she replied with a new acerbity.

'Yes you do,' he said, feeling foolish as soon as he had said it.

Alfred began to walk with a stick, not all the time and only with reluctance. When he was especially in pain and she would hand him his stick, he would refuse it angrily, saying that he did not need it, even if he did; and when, later, he took it surreptitiously in the hope she would not notice, she said, with a hint of malicious triumph, 'So you do need it.'

'Not when you first gave it to me,' he replied petulantly. 'I made a bad move, and that set the pain off.'

'If that's what you say.'

'It is what I say.'

Shortly afterwards there occurred an incident, trivial in itself, that marked a turning in their relations: she put parsley on his boiled potatoes. It so happened that Alfred detested parsley on boiled potatoes.

'I've told you before,' he said, that you shouldn't put parsley on boiled potatoes. Potatoes have a subtle taste and parsley overwhelms it.' Therefore, objectively-speaking, it was wrong to put parsley on boiled potatoes. It was a matter of fact rather than of taste.

'Everyone puts parsley on boiled potatoes,' said Bridget.

'Everyone said the earth was flat and the sun went round it,' said Alfred, the Copernicus of boiled potatoes. He was furious that she was obliging him to utter such commonplaces.

For a couple of weeks afterwards, there was no parsley on the boiled potatoes, but then it made its appearance again. Alfred was beside himself. He flung the stick down that he had brought to the table.

'How many times do I have to tell you?' he asked. 'No parsley on the potatoes!'

His instructions on the matter could hardly have been clearer. Could Bridget not understand plain English? It is true that she had hardly been the brightest product of the secretarial college she had attended, itself of a low standard, but even she should have been able to follow simple instructions.

'I like parsley' she said.

'Liking it or not liking it is not the point,' said Alfred. 'I've told you that it masks the flavour of potatoes.'

But the parsley problem was only the beginning. Bridget increasingly defied what she thought of as Alfred's whims, but Alfred thought of as rational choices. She would not listen to reason: she repeated her disregard of his instructions more and more often. It began to take on the aspect of a campaign against him.

He retreated as much as he could into the garden. Some days, however, it rained, and damp was very bad for his arthritis. But even in the garden, when the practical matter in hand distracted him from his unpleasant thoughts, she managed to interfere and destroy his peace. She deliberately brought him tea that was too strong or too weak, or called him to lunch before he was ready, in the middle of some important task, or alternatively delayed it until he had lost his appetite. She knew his likes and dislikes, and acted accordingly.

She started to give him sandwiches instead of cooked meals, and sandwiches moreover made of bad bread that she knew he detested. In Alfred's opinion, this was a clear breach of the implicit contract between them: he paid, she looked after him. What else, indeed, was she there for? She was becoming less ornamental by the day, thanks to ageing and a propensity to let herself go. She would stay all day in her dressing gown, her hair disarranged. She would spend hours on the telephone without telling him who she was speaking to, or what about. If he asked, she simply replied 'A friend,' or 'Nothing much.' How could she really talk for so long? If you emptied the entire content of Bridget's brain, it would not fill more than a quarter of an hour at most. Certainly Alfred had never had an intelligent conversation with her.

Her demands for money, supposedly for housekeeping, began to increase, faster, Alfred supposed, than the rate of inflation. There was no explanation other than that she was keeping money aside for herself: certainly, the quantity and quality of the food that she bought declined as she asked for more money. Everything she bought was now of the cheapest. At first, he attributed this to nostalgia for her humble origins: you could take the bourgeois out of the plebeian but not the plebeian out of the bourgeois, And while he admired the proletariat as a class, he had nothing but contempt for the plebeian as a person.

The money that Bridget now demanded certainly did not go on clothes, the most frequent destination of plebeian defalcations. Nor did she spend it on holidays or excursions for herself, because she took none. Indeed, Alfred began sometimes to wish that she would take them, to relieve the tension in the house. She didn't drink in secret, nor did she gamble. There was only one conclusion to be drawn; and while Alfred had never concerned himself much over money, the house was large and expensive to run, inflation was eating into his capital that he had invested too cautiously on the assumption that money would retain its value, and Bridget was demanding weekly sums in excess of his income. This could not continue.

At the same time, Bridget grew defiant. She filled the house with teddy bears, which Alfred abominated but which she would not remove. She had the television on all day, tuned to the worst banalities, even when she was not looking at it. When Alfred objected, and made disdainful remarks, she said it was a bit of company for her. She claimed that the house was her domain as the garden was his; but increasingly this was an unequal division, for as his arthritis grew worse, so he was obliged to spend more time indoors. In the past, when trying to educate his female companions politically, he would quote his favourite dictum, that freedom was the recognition of necessity, but nothing was now further from his mind.

He had now only to say that he detested something for Bridget to do or cherish it. But despite their manifest inefficacy, he continued to employ disdain, reproach, criticism and recrimination to change her conduct, for they still possessed gratification in themselves. No man feels entirely deprived of purpose while reprehending or despising others.

Now there was war between them, with provocation on one side and rising to the bait on the other. It never occurred to Alfred that Bridget, uneducated and ignorant as she had been when he met her, could be a strategist. As far as he was concerned, she was the kind of person who simply responded to circumstances, as an amoeba responds to the chemicals in its immediate environment.

Bridget served vegetables that were either nearly raw and upset Alfred's stomach or so overcooked that they were little more than indistinguishable mush. It was not possible that this was entirely by accident: no human being could be so entirely lacking in intelligence as that. One day, provoked beyond endurance, Alfred struck out at her with his stick, as hard as he was able.

There was a bruise on her forearm. She rose from the table, put on her coat and rushed from the house. She returned an hour or two later.

'Where have you been?' asked Alfred.

'To the doctor's.'

'What for?'

A slight smile or grimace played on Bridget's face.

'That's between me and the doctor,' she said.

Alfred was uneasy.

'There was no need,' he said.

'Not for you, perhaps, but for me.'

The doctor had given her some pills to calm her down, which she did not need. She kept them as evidence, though.

Some time later, Alfred broached the subject of moving from the house. He could no longer manage the garden, which was therefore going to seed, and the house had always been much larger than they needed. No one visited them, or ever would, it was expensive to keep up and it gave Bridget a lot of unnecessary work. Perhaps that was why her face had settled into a fixed expression of bitterness.

'I don't want to move, I like it here' said Bridget, though her expression belied her words, which she spoke through clenched teeth. Alfred did not know that, while out shopping one day, she had consulted a lawyer.

She continued to irritate him in ways that others, but not Alfred, might have considered small. The problem with founding your tastes, likes and dislikes, on the laws of the universe (as Alfred believed his to be) was that deviation from them was an offence against reason itself, and therefore a proper reason for anger. His anger was now so frequently aroused that, for the first time in his life, it gave him no pleasure.

He began to recall Felicity with something like affection. They were not divorced and he still paid her maintenance. This sometimes necessitated communication between them, and though for their last years together they had barely spoken, they gradually found that it was easy to talk about more than the mere matter in hand. They spoke of the children, of course; they had in common their somewhat distant relations with both of them. They spoke of other members of Alfred's family with whom Felicity had remained in friendlier contact than Alfred had ever managed. They spoke sometimes even of the lamentable inflation that threatened their standard of living, when they were at a time of life when they could do nothing about it. They even spoke of the old days as if they had been happy. But Alfred revealed nothing of his present situation, for that would have been to admit error.

Meanwhile, Bridget grew ever bolder or more aggressive in her disregard of Alfred's wishes and orders. Indeed, she seemed often to carry out his orders in mirror-image form.

'You know I detest those slippers!' said Alfred, pointing to feet covered, to all appearance, by fluffy nylon pandas.

'Well I like them.'

This was her answer to everything: I like this, I like that, I like them. Was it worse if she really did, or was only saying it to annoy him? She never considered what he liked or wanted. You might have thought she was living on her own, with only herself to please.

To begin with, at least, she had done her work as a house-wife, if anything displaying obsessive tendencies in her pursuit of settling dust. But gradually this had changed: her over-conscientiousness had changed by degrees into slovenliness; washing was not done and she began to insist that Alfred should wear the same shirt on three or four successive days, whereas before she had insisted that he change it every day. Moreover, even when she washed a shirt, she would no longer iron it. She said he could iron shirts himself if he wanted them ironed; there was no point in making work because he never went anywhere anyway. His bed went unmade and unchanged; they no longer ate together or at the same table: the times when they were hungry no longer coincided. Alfred began to prepare his own food, and though this ensured that it was cooked correctly, he had no control over the ingredients he was able to use, as it was she who bought everything and took no notice of what he wanted.

She was like a domestic guerrilla. Blessed with no imagination, never having expressed an interesting idea in her life (and incapable even of recognising one), she was nevertheless inventive of ways of aggravating him. She would either leave windows open until all the heat in a room had escaped or heat them to boiling point. She would play cheap music at maximum volume so that it was inescapable; she appeared never to tire of the inane chatter on the wireless turned to a station that specialised in it. If Alfred turned it, or the television, off, she turned it back on within a minute or two; if Alfred tried to listen to Beethoven, she drowned it out until he could stand the discord no more.

Alfred decided that anything was better than to continue this mode of life. One day, when she had particularly irritated him, he said:

'You're making my life hell. You'll have to go.'

'Why me?'

'Because you're the one doing it.'

'Go where?'

'Anywhere.'

'Who'll look after you?'

It was true that, despite everything, he was increasingly dependent on her. Some days his arthritis was so bad that he could not unscrew a jar; his grip was now very weak. It was dangerous for him to drive because he could scarcely turn his head to the right or to the left when he pulled up at a junction. He had always been an aggressive driver, but now he was both aggressive and indecisive.

'It would cost a fortune to pay someone to do all that I do for you,' said Bridget.

'Cheap at twice the price,' said Alfred.

That was the end of the discussion – for now. But the subject of separation came up more and more often between them.

'When do you want to go?' asked Alfred, exasperated beyond endurance (or so he thought).

'I'm not going,' said Bridget. It was not time yet, though the time would come.

Once Alfred even tried a conciliatory tone. But as soon as it emerged from his mouth, he knew that it sounded bogus and was moreover a tactical mistake. It made him sound weak. He did not repeat the experiment.

'I'm not prepared to put up with this any longer,' he said one day, after Bridget served him up with a sandwich of dried up bread, curling at the edges as only sliced packaged bread could, and a tinned sardine.

'What are you going to do about it?' asked Bridget insolently.

Alfred took his stick and swept everything from the table with it. Things scattered on the floor and a plate smashed. Bridget took out her camera and took a photograph of the result.

'Why are you taking a photograph of that for?' asked Alfred.

'Evidence.'

'What of?'

'Your bad temper, your unreasonableness, your violence.'

A few days later, Bridget said to him:

'I'll go if you make it worth my while.'

'What do you want?' asked Alfred.

'The house and sixty per cent of your pension.'

'For God's sake be reasonable. You can have half the house.'

'The whole house or I'm not going.'

Alfred would be impoverished if Bridget had her way.

'You can't sell the house with me in it, unless I agree to go,' she said. 'I've checked.' If he wanted to be rid of her, he had two choices: to go himself, in which case it would be deemed as desertion (they had lived long enough together to be counted as married) or agree to her conditions. 'And,' she added, 'I've got the doctor's record.'

The lawyer had told her that with such a record no court would be sympathetic to Alfred in the allocation of assets. She would tell the court with a catch or sob in her voice that he had been violent to her on numerous occasions, and it would believe her. And she knew that she was good at sobbing when required.

The price for her departure being still too high, Alfred tried to continue as before, but the situation only worsened. Her hostility to him was now perfectly open, concealed only if there were a third party present, which was rarely, when she would suddenly appear solicitous of his welfare. She was establishing a case should it ever be necessary.

The contrast between Bridget the vengeful harridan and Bridget the saintly companion-cum-nurse etched itself painfully into Alfred's mind. To be the virtual prisoner of a person very much less intelligent than oneself, who would not even know the date of the start of the French Revolution, and took no notice of anything but her own tiny concerns, was to Alfred a peculiar torture. It was humiliating; it was unjust.

However much or hard he thought about it, Alfred could find no solution. The philosophy that had explained to him so early in his life the workings of the universe and the whole of human history was of no help whatever to him. He turned the same thoughts over and over in his mind, but never made any advance on them. They added boredom to all his miseries. There was no solution, or at least none that was satisfactory.

Worse still, and with increasing frequency, he had to call upon her assistance for the performance of the tasks that youth takes for granted, for example to button his shirt or tie his shoes. Bridget performed these tasks, but with malice and ill-grace. She would pull him about as if he were a sullen or resistive schoolchild, or an inanimate object of awkward shape. She would accuse him of being uncooperative.

'For God's sake, keep still,' she would say. 'How am I supposed to do it with you fidgeting about like a baby?'

To protest that he had not moved, that he was keeping still, would have sounded feeble; but not to protest was to admit the truth of the reproach. Bridget was not very bright, but she was acute: shrewd, Alfred reflected, as all people of her degraded class were.

One day, while helping him to dress, Bridget struck him across the face. It was a light blow and left no mark; there was no one to whom he could complain, and no evidence that it had ever been struck. In any case, to admit that a woman had hit him would have been humiliating. In addition, therefore, to all his other feelings about her, he began to feel physically afraid of her. This was a humiliation too far: all his adult life, he had inspired fear rather than felt it. He had never been a physical coward: in his youth, he had even been something of a boxer, always emerging (at least in his memory) victorious from his bouts. Now with his arthritis, he was defenceless, and likely to remain so. The question had to be settled once and for all.

He agreed to her conditions. She did not trust him merely to keep to his word: she insisted on a legal agreement. Only then could the house be put up for sale.

Bridget expressed no interest in the question of Alfred's future, where he should go and how he should manage. She was in a hurry to go, and go she did. Her one act of assistance to him was to buy him the local newspaper in which were advertised homes for the elderly who needed assistance in everyday tasks.

Alfred moved into a little brick bungalow, half of which was his domain (the other half belonged to an old lady who did not know who she was). There were twenty such bungalows in a little cluster, with hardly any space between them; there was a community hall in which people could sit round the walls like wallflowers at a dance, or indulge in sing-songs or bingo led by a community worker of the most determined jollity. In addition, the hall smelled permanently of the air-fresheners used unsuccessfully to disguise the odour of urine, which had names such as Meadow Flowers, Spring Sunshine, Ocean Breeze and Forest Fruit. Alfred had always had a horror of the promiscuous egalitarianism of social life, and therefore held himself apart from all the other residents of the bungalows.

His income was now very small, smaller than his obligations to Felicity. He had to eat into his capital, small as it now was.

He saw no one except the member of staff whose job it was to check the residents had not died overnight and to help with washing, dressing and shopping. One of his sons visited every few weeks, staying as briefly as possible on the pretext that he had come a long way and had to get back, as he was very busy the next day. He found the state into which his father had declined both depressing and embarrassing, especially the latter; as soon as he arrived, therefore, he made clear (though not in so many words) that he was anxious to go. His manner was distant and his conversation forced.

Almost his only contact with the world outside the Homestead Retirement Village, as it called itself, was now with Felicity by telephone, whose virtues and qualities he almost acknowledged in the privacy of his own mind. She had been the most intelligent and upright, as well as best-looking of all his consorts and mistresses. She had remained single since their separation, which Alfred now interpreted as flattering to himself. He even let the thought to total reconciliation flicker through his mind, though of course he could not be expected to make the first move in that direction. But for the first time in his life, his conversation was not didactic; it was almost a dialogue.

Then he fell ill, and sensed at once that it was an illness from which he could not recover. All his life he had preached that death was a normal and natural event and therefore nothing to rail against or even fear. When his cancer was diagnosed and he was offered not a curative but a palliative operation, he turned it down.

His consolation now was to plan his funeral arrangements. Despite his lifelong materialism, he imagined himself present, in some immaterial form, at that event, hovering above the mourners and observing them. It would not be a religious ceremony, of course: no need for illusions. Once you were gone, you were gone, apart from this brief hovering moment; still he felt obliged to give his son funeral directions once the prognosis was clear. These included the number and contents of the sandwiches to be served after the cremation.

'There will be twenty people,' he said. 'Two sausage rolls each, that makes forty, and four cheese or ham sandwiches, say forty of each. Ten or twelve of the guests will have a glass of wine. Two bottles of red and two of white should be more than enough.'

His son knew that there would not be twenty: six would be more like it. He said nothing, except that he would see to it that his father's instructions were carried out.

Alfred was moved to a hospice for the dying. He was now so weak that he could hardly lift his head from the pillow. His son, who visited him for a last time, wondered whether it was the drugs he was given or the illness itself that caused Alfred's state of mind.

During one of the clearings in his mental mist, Alfred said: 'Tell your mother than she can come to see me if she likes.'

That night, Alfred's son relayed the message to his mother. 'Tell your father I'll come if he wants me to,' she said.

But there was no time left for negotiation. Alfred died two days later. There were four people at his funeral and a few sandwiches left over.

A Poisoned Existence

E DGAR WILLIAMS was a retired history teacher. He had spent his entire career at the same boarding school, where his wife had been the school 'nurse', in charge of what had been called, rather grandly, the Infirmary. He told each class that he taught that it was the worst in his entire experience. While not logically impossible, this was improbable; and in fact he was fortunate that the school had been one in which the pupils had in general behaved well and had always wanted to learn. He had been a dedicated pedagogue, and he had always found the induction of young minds into the pleasures and importance of knowledge of the past deeply gratifying. He never regretted his choice of career and at his retirement there had been a moving farewell attended by a number of old pupils some of whom were now middle-aged themselves and had had distinguished careers. They clubbed together to give him a handsome early edition of Gibbon as a retirement present. He was both happy and sad.

His wife's work had never been very onerous. Unusually for her time, she had a university degree, but had never used it. She had found the prospect of keeping her husband's home, making jam, having time to read, and a little pastoral work among the children a perfectly satisfying prospect. They had never been rich, of course, but at least at first his teacher's salary had been enough to live on, and genteel poverty was still a possible way of life. But now a shabby old age with an inadequate pension faced them, prices not only having risen, but disproportionately to one another, and necessities having seemed to grow more numerous. Their one son, also a teacher, as in no position to help them, even though his wife worked. They had a baby and lived far off. In any case, pride would not have permitted them to accept help from him even had he been in a position to offer it.

A historian is not a proper historian unless he has done some original research and published it. Mr Williams had always been aware of this, and though in general he had been happy and content in his work, it had always been his intention in retirement to conduct such research. Until then, his only appearance in print had been a few articles in the school magazine about the founder of the school, a seventeenth century wool merchant, derived mainly from secondary sources. They were what he called, auto-derisively, 'scissors and paste jobs'.

His ambitions for real research were modest. He intended no grand narrative of the fate of nations or whole continents, no revisionary theory. It was too late, and he was not qualified, for that, and in any case he was drawn by nature more to the small change of life rather than to its grander aspects or panoramas (though, of course, he had had to teach these). In any case, he could not afford to travel far, not even by train; he would therefore confine himself to local history. If anyone accused him of wasting his time on mere footnotes to history, he would reply – he had the answer ready – that life itself consisted of an accumulation or succession of footnotes. It was not only great events that counted in people's lives, but small events and changes in manners: in fact, they counted more. He decided to examine the birth-rate in his parish during the Seventeenth Century. Was the pattern pre-modern, early-modern, or just plain modern? The parish records had long since been removed to the county archives, but fortunately the county town was not far away and there was a bus service most days.

Mrs Williams thought her husband's plan a good one. It would hardly bring fame or fortune – perhaps an article or two in an obscure journal – but an active man could not retire from life as well as from his job. When he took himself off to the archives, she made him sandwiches and got on with her own chores. When he returned, she asked him how he had got on and he replied that the work was progressing.

But increasingly this was not true. The archive staff were very good and seemed never to tire of his requests: no one becomes an archivist except from love of documents with the intensity of a secret vice. Old handwriting is often difficult to decipher – no one wrote parish records with the convenience in mind of researchers four centuries later – but Mr Williams' increasing difficulties did not lie there. The old parish records would be open before him, his pen and notebook would be at the ready, his pen hovering… but somehow nothing would transfer itself, via his mind, from the records to the notebook. He stared at the records, which came into and went out of focus: he could not fix his mind on them. Instead, there was a curious blankness in his head, as though his brain had been replaced by a vacuum. His blank periods were at first short, and he could persuade himself that they would pass, and indeed he could shake himself from them as one shakes water from an umbrella after coming in from the rain. But the blank periods became longer and impossible to shake off by mere effort. A few times an archivist approached him while he stared into space and asked him whether he was all right.

He confessed to his wife that his work was going much slower than he had expected. When she asked why, he said that some of the archivists were being deliberately obstructive, the records were more disorganised than he had ever supposed, and possibly he would need new glasses to decipher the writing: though, as far as she knew, he had made no efforts to see an optician.

Mrs Williams noticed that he was taking longer to prepare himself to go to the archives. We all slow down with age, that is natural, but this was different. Nor was his slowness a kind of reluctance, like that of a schoolboy creeping unwillingly to school. He appeared to have difficulty in gathering his things and then in keeping them together. She would reassemble them for him and then he would go through them anxiously, misplacing them again so that they would have to be gathered again. He had always been somewhat fussy and punctilious about small matters – rubbers had to be of a certain size, ink of a certain colour, and so forth – but this was something new and different. He misplaced things and then, when found, puzzled as to what they were and why he needed them.

He continued to go to the archives, but achieved less and less there. The staff knew him and knew what he was supposedly working on, and placed documents before him as usual; but more and more he just stared into space or looked at the pages with puzzlement, as if not understanding what they were or why they had been brought.

Why was he like this, he asked himself in his more lucid moments?

It must be the sandwiches: his wife, Muriel, was putting something in them, arsenic most probably. Arsenic was tasteless and easily mixed in with other things, such as butter. It was also a cumulative poison, so that it was only to be expected that he should deteriorate over time. He had never had a day's illness in his life before (apart from the childhood diseases now conquered by vaccination), so why should he now be unwell? It stood to reason, there was no other possible explanation.

But why should Muriel want to poison him? She had always been a good wife and he had noticed no change in her attitude to him. And yet he knew that, even after many years together, some of his own thoughts and feelings were hidden from her. Was it not likely, therefore, certain even, that some of her thoughts and feelings were hidden from him? There was no point in asking her, for if someone were poisoning you, he or she would hardly admit to it on questioning. It was best not to let her know that he knew what she was doing. He would continue to take his sandwiches with him every time he went to the archives, but he would not eat them.

Not that this was the perfect solution because one day it came to him in a flash: if she were poisoning the sandwiches, might she not be poisoning everything else she prepared for him? It would be more difficult to avoid the poison at home. It would not be possible to avoid it altogether, for then she would know that he knew; but since the danger of arsenic was proportionate to the quantity taken, he might take so little as to render it almost harmless.

There remained the puzzle as to why she was doing it. She did not love another man, of that he could be sure. No, it must be money. He had taken out life insurance many years earlier, on which there was a bonus for dying earlier than the life tables suggested. It is true that Muriel had never shown much interest in money, but perhaps she resented having less money than, say, a plumber or an electrician. This was a reversal of the natural order of things, according to which the better-educated should earn more than the worse-educated. Perhaps, too, she blamed him for having been only a schoolmaster when, with a bit of effort, he might have done something more lucrative.

It is not easy to disguise from your wife your belief that she is poisoning you; and it is even more difficult in practice to dispose of the food that she has prepared for you without her noticing. Mrs Williams – Muriel – noticed that Mr Williams – Edgar – had changed in his attitude towards her, though she could not put her finger on exactly how, let alone why. He seemed to be almost wary of her: not that he had ever been very demonstrative in his affections, which he had supposed she took as read. The change made no sense.

Clear or thin soup he could sometimes dispose of in the pots of potted plants to which his wife was devoted. He bought some little plastic bags into which he slipped the food when Muriel left the room, putting them into the pockets of his tweed jacket (he had worn tweed jackets, usually with leather patches, all his adult life, and continued to do so now). Then he would sneak out to the dustbin and try to secrete them there, burying them in the rubbish already in the bin. He was like an alcoholic who tries to hide the evidence of his habit.

But of course Muriel noticed, at first that he was not eating and then that he was disposing of the food in this strange way. She thought at first that he must be protecting her from knowledge of his loss of appetite caused by a hidden and presumably serious disease, in other words cancer.

'Is there anything wrong with you, Edgar?' she asked.

'No, why do you ask?' His eyes darted about strangely.

'You don't seem to be eating anything.'

It was true that he was losing weight, but it was not quite true that he was eating nothing. He would eat – in secret – from previously unopened packets of biscuits and the like; but he had to discard what he did not eat there and then, for otherwise Muriel might tamper with it. He was reasonably sure that she was too inexperienced a poisoner to introduce poison into an unopened packet.

'I don't feel very hungry these days,' said Edgar. 'There's nothing else wrong.'

'Are you sure?' asked Muriel.

'Yes of course,' said Edgar, mildly irritated by the question's hypocrisy. First you poison someone, then you express concern for how he is! Perhaps she was trying to find out whether the poison was working; well, he wouldn't give her that satisfaction. There were dangers, no doubt, to not telling her anything, or telling her that he had no symptoms, for then she would increase the dose, as anyone would who was poisoning someone without apparent effect. Poison had always been a woman's weapon. Muriel, he decided, was the Madame de Brinvilliers of their village. It was strange how women's methods did not change down the ages. If it hadn't been so serious, Edgar might have laughed at the unoriginality of it all. Then he thought that it was just as well that he knew his history.

'I think you ought to go and see Dr Smith,' said Muriel.

'There's no need,' said Edgar. 'Stop fussing.'

Actually, he began to think it might not be a bad idea to consult Dr Smith. He could measure the level of arsenic in his blood, or rather (Edgar liked to be strictly accurate) have it measured. But he wouldn't disclose to Muriel that he was going to see the doctor because she might insist on coming with him so that he could not speak freely. Nor would he telephone for an appointment in case she overheard.

Instead of going to the county archive, one day he went to Dr Smith's surgery.

'I want an appointment to see the doctor,' he said to the receptionist, who regarded it as her job to protect Dr Smith from more work than necessary.

'Is it urgent?' she asked.

'Fairly,' replied Edgar. It had been going on for quite a long time now, and he could not positively say that Muriel would succeed in the next few days; but you never knew with arsenic, she might suddenly give him a fatal dose. However vigilant he was, she might succeed in putting it in, say, his toothpaste. It had been careless of him, in fact, not to have thought of that before. The danger was not only from food and drink.

'What's wrong with you?' asked the receptionist.

Surely that was a matter between him and Dr Smith?

'It's confidential.'

The receptionist, who had a dim view of humanity, thought it must be something venereal. Tweed jackets with leather patches might be deceptive: all men were fundamentally alike. Everyone was the same, when you got down to it.

'Are you quite sure it's Dr Smith you need to see?' she asked, with a hint of satire in her voice.

'Quite,' said Edgar.

The receptionist sighed. It was only wasting time: Dr Smith would only pass him on to the Clinic.

'All right,' she said, with the air of one whose good advice has been spurned. 'Next Wednesday, at ten o'clock.'

But Edgar failed to keep the appointment, not because he was feeling better, but because he mistook Wednesday for Tuesday, as he sometimes did these days. The receptionist rang to ask why he had not kept his appointment, and it was Muriel who answered the call.

'You didn't tell me you had an appointment at the doctor's,' she said to him when he returned from the archives, unaware that he had missed it. Her tone was mildly accusatory.

'It's for Wednesday,' he said.

'Today is Wednesday,' said Muriel. 'What's wrong with you,

Edgar?'

'We all make mistakes.'

'I think I'd better make another appointment,' said Muriel, 'and come with you.'

When Edgar was called into the doctor's room – 'Edgar Williams!' – Muriel entered with him.

'I want to make sure you tell the doctor everything,' said Muriel.

Oh, she was clever, Muriel. That way she would make sure that the doctor did not find out that she was poisoning him.

Edgar, cornered, told the doctor that he had been feeling under the weather for some time, but that there were no specific symptoms of which he could complain. Muriel told the doctor of his loss of appetite, his weight loss, and his unaccustomed propensity to lose things. Despite Edgar's denial of any pain or discomfort, the doctor thought that, at his age, he might have cancer, and sent him for tests.

'It was just as well I came with you,' said Muriel on the way home, 'or you'd have told the doctor nothing.'

She went with him to see the specialist as well, but this time her plan to prevent him from revealing what she was doing to him was thwarted: when it came to the consultation, the specialist wanted to see Edgar on his own.

As soon as the doctor had finished examining him and Edgar had put on his clothes again, Edgar felt freer to speak. He put the flat of his hand over his mouth to prevent his words from spreading too far. They were for the doctor's ears only.

'Doctor,' he said, 'my wife's poisoning me.'

The doctor, who had been about to say that, as far as he was concerned, Edgar had a clean bill of health, was professional enough to conceal his surprise.

'How?' he asked simply.

'Arsenic,' replied Edgar. 'She puts it in everything.'

'How do you know?'

'I feel it. She's changed towards me.'

'In what way?'

'She's furtive. She won't look me in the eye. Everything tastes different. I don't feel well. I'm tired. I can't think. I can't concentrate like I used to.'

None of this was evidence of poisoning, of course; but if you thought it was, mere argument would not persuade you otherwise. It was clear that Edgar needed another kind of doctor.

'You can measure arsenic in the blood, can't you doctor?' asked Edgar.

'Yes, easily,' he replied. Well why not, if it would reassure him, or at least cause him not to complain? And after all, it would be disastrous – humiliating – if a patient who told him that he was being poisoned subsequently died of poisoning without having had a simple blood test performed on him. The doctor would never live it down: the man who missed arsenic poisoning.

'After the test, I'll ask one of my colleagues to see you,' he said. 'He'll send you an appointment.'

Muriel asked Edgar what the doctor had told him.

'Nothing very much. He ordered some tests, I think, and suggested I saw someone else.'

'Who?'

Edgar had either forgotten or forgotten to ask, he couldn't remember which. A toxicologist, he supposed, a specialist in poisons, but he didn't let on that they were on Muriel's trail. Edgar had always (guiltily) been fond of detective stories, and he had learned from them that it was a cardinal error of detection to reveal too soon that one suspected the suspect.

To Edgar's surprise, the second specialist seemed hardly interested in the effects of the poison, as if he took them for granted. His questions on this important aspect of the case were at most perfunctory. By contrast, he took an almost obsessive interest in the time, the date and the year, and the fact that Edgar was unsure of them. The fact that Edgar could not recall the exact location of the consultation seemed to be of greater importance to him than that Edgar was being slowly murdered by his wife. Edgar found it most unsatisfactory.

The specialist understood nothing. He insisted on talking to Muriel, which led Edgar to suppose that he must be in league with her. They spoke together – he could hear them whispering conspiratorially – for a very long time. What about?

They returned home in silence, broke eventually by Muriel.

'How could you think that, Edgar?'

'Think what?'

'That I am poisoning you.'

How do you explain to a poisoner the reasons you think she is poisoning you?

'What makes you think it? Why should I be doing it?'

'I don't know, Muriel. Only you can say that.'

The second specialist had prescribed some pills for Edgar to take, though obviously he would not take them. The doctor was in league with his wife, and it was she who handed him the pills to take. Moreover, they were capsules, perfect for tampering with. But for the sake of peace, he pretended sometimes to take them; he slid them between his cheek and his gum to spit them out later when Muriel wasn't looking. It amused him, in a way, to do this, and took him back to his childhood, when he would spit out the horrible things that they gave him for his own good. At least untaken pills were easier to conceal than uneaten meals.

He stopped going to the archives. At first, he went occasionally, and then not at all. It was not so much that there was no point in going as that he forgot to go. Instead, he would take a walk that lasted about fifteen minutes and that followed the same route. One day, however, he was lost and it was the police who found him walking along the main road out of the village. He could not explain to them why he was there or where he was going. It was even an effort for him to explain where he had come from. The police returned him home; from then on, Muriel would not allow him out on his own.

He was confined to the house. It was the first time that he and his wife spent twenty-four hours a day in each other's company. Previously they had always been busy with their own occupations, but now looking after him was Muriel's sole occupation. And he was much diminished.

He still believed that she was poisoning him, however, even if hunger sometimes got the better of his fear. If Muriel urged him to eat, it was because she wanted him to absorb some poison; if she did not, it was because she had poisoned something else. But somehow the conviction with which he held these beliefs, or the importance he ascribed to them, began to wane.

Muriel imprisoned him, but he imprisoned Muriel. She still went to the shops, but as quickly as possible in case he wandered away in the meantime. Strictly speaking, she should not have left him for a moment, but that was a counsel of perfection. She never went out, though, without fearing what she might find on her return.

Dementia, the doctor had told her, albeit in its early stages: but it could only get worse. Some with the disease were contented with their lot, in a fatuous way, but others became querulous or paranoid, remaining so until they were no longer capable of any mentation at all, and that is what was happening to Edgar. He remembered that he was being poisoned, but not what he had had for breakfast.

Edgar sat in his armchair all day. Muriel would bring him tea on a tray and sometimes he would wave it away imperiously, or mutter Poison! Sometimes, though, he would drink it.

Muriel began to have a problem of her own. It was her hip. It was painful in whatever pose she took. It prevented her from sleeping. She tried lying on one side and then the other, but there was no comfortable position. It made walking difficult and excruciating.

She went to the doctor and he ordered an x-ray. The arthritis was very far advanced. The only solution was for the hip to be replaced by operation.

But there was a long wait. She was not a priority, the surgeon said, because unfortunately (yes, that was the word he used), her condition was not a life-threatening one, and there were always more urgent cases to attend to. No torturer, however, could have devised a torture more painful than to send out someone to shop with such a hip. Muriel's face turned grey with pain.

Then Edgar began to lose control of his bladder, infrequently at first, then more often, and without realising that he had done so. This increased the quantity of washing to be done. The house took on a permanent odour of urine and detergent. Fortunately, the senses soon grow dulled to any sensation, and soon only visitors noticed – or would have noticed, had there been any.

Muriel needed help, she told the doctor, she couldn't go on like this. He gave her some pills to cheer her up, but they did no good. He, the doctor, had gained some time, and gaining time was one of the main aims of his practice. He was often more like a juggler than a healer: his patients were like balls in the air (some were flaming torches) whom he had to somehow keep from crashing to the ground.

Before any assistance for Muriel could be arranged – in the form of a fat lady who was to come once a week to help her with the copious washing occasioned by incontinence – she was called suddenly to the hospital for her operation. After having waited many long months, she was told peremptorily by telephone to present herself at the hospital next morning at seven o'clock.

'What about my husband?' she asked. 'I can't just leave him.'

The admissions clerk knew nothing of her husband, and he was not her department.

'I don't know anything about him,' she said.

'He's unwell,' Muriel said. 'He can't look after himself.'

'Well if you don't want your operation…' said the clerk, as if Muriel were being difficult.

'It's not that I don't want my operation,' said Muriel. 'I do, I'm in agony. But my husband…'

'You'll have to speak to your GP or social services about him. You must make up your mind: shall I put you down for tomorrow or not? There are plenty of others who have been waiting just as long as you.'

'Put me down,' said Muriel.

'Do you need hospital transport?'

'Yes, I'd like that.'

She'd like it? Did she think that the hospital was running some kind of pleasure resort?

'The car'll call for you at six-thirty,' said the clerk with some asperity. Of course, no one really likes to have to be ready for six-thirty, and the clerk informed people of the need with a slight frisson of pleasure, whose origin she did not analyse. It was especially gratifying with these hoity-toity types like Mrs Williams, or Muriel as she had first addressed her when she answered.

Now Muriel had to make swift arrangements for Edgar. Never having been one for domestic tasks, scarcely able even to boil an egg at the height of his domestic abilities, he could not possibly stay at home while she was in hospital. He would have to go somewhere. She phoned the doctor's surgery.

'Greengage Surgery, hold the line please.'

The line went dead. Was there still anyone there? Difficult to say. Should Muriel ring off and try again? She decided to hang on and was eventually rewarded.

'Greengage Surgery, thank you for waiting.'

'I'm Mrs Williams, Mrs Muriel Williams. I'm calling about my husband, Edgar.'

'Edgar who?'

'Edgar Williams, of course. He's my husband.'

'These days you never know.'

'Is it urgent?'

'Yes, I need to speak to the doctor.'

'What about?'

The telephonist said she needed to know, so that she could decide whether or not to pass on the message urgently. She decided that it was relatively urgent, and would pass on the massage to the doctor, who would call back.

Time seemed to accelerate while Muriel waited because there wasn't much of it. Had she cast a message in a bottle, as it were, into the vastness of the Pacific? Each moment that passed was a moment of doubt. The longer it went on, the more acute the doubt. But then the doctor did call back, and immediately grasped the urgency of the situation. The only solution he could think of was to admit Edgar to hospital for what he called E.R.C., Emergency Respite Care. It would have to be to another hospital from Muriel's, of course; regrettable, but there was no choice.

A car came to take Edgar away. Muriel tried to explain to him where he was going and why, but he could not grasp it. She explained as well as possible why she could not accompany him. Anyway, no one really wants his poisoner with him.

A little after Edgar had departed, Muriel's hospital telephoned to say that, owing to unforeseen circumstances, her operation had been postponed to another day, as yet unspecified. She would be fitted in as soon as possible, but there was no way of knowing when that would be.

Muriel tried to retrieve Edgar from Freshfields District Hospital, to which he had been taken, but it proved impossible. It was as if an inexorable giant machine had been set in motion and there was no stopping it.

Once admitted to Elizabeth Fry Ward, Edgar was bewildered. Where was he, what were all these people around him doing? Two young men, dressed in a white outfit, speaking a fluent but inaccurate English with a strange accent, stripped him of his clothes, dressed him in some ill-fitting flannel pyjamas and put him to bed.

In the bed next to his was an old man who muttered more or less continually. Edgar took no notice of him.

When they brought Edgar food, leaving it sometimes barely within reach, he played with it rather than ate it. Even when a nurse tried to encourage him to eat it, he refused like a little boy refusing his greens. He would put a morsel in his mouth and wait for it to dissolve rather than chew and swallow it.

'Come on Edgar,' said the nurse, a fat and jolly Nigerian. 'We haven't got all day. There are plenty of other patients. It isn't poisoned,' she added, laughing.

But it was, of course. That was why he pushed the food away. The nurse gave up; no one dies of missing a meal and it was true that there were many other patients to see to.

At six o'clock, with darkness falling, Edgar was given his sleeping draught. He was just the kind of man – confused and disorientated – who would try to get out of bed and start wandering without purpose, being found dead on the stairs the next morning (Elizabeth Fry Ward was on the seventh floor); so in addition to his sleeping draught, they affixed stainless steel bars to the side of his bed to imprison him safely in it. Even this had its inconveniences, for he could rattle them constantly through the night, disturbing the nurse who was trying to finish the paperwork on her desk and then file her nails.

The doctor came the next morning and decided that Edgar needed an infusion because he had not been drinking enough and was now dehydrated. There followed something of a duel between Edgar and the staff as he tried repeatedly to remove the tube whose purpose he did not understand. He pulled it out and they replaced it; he pulled it out again and they replaced it again. Before long, they bandaged his arm and also the hand with which he tried to remove the tube. But none of this prevented him from pushing away the poisoned food that they offered him.

Later that day, Edgar had a severe fit at the end of which he died. Dramatic, if somewhat perfunctory, efforts were made to revive him but they failed, and were made for form's sake, just in case anyone asked afterwards whether they had been made. What, after all, was the point of continuing a life such as his, with its inevitable decline into an ever more vegetative state?

Muriel was informed by telephone of Edgar's unexpected demise by no less a person than the hospital's Director of Nursing Affairs, who expressed her profound regret and deepest condolences. The hospital had discovered that such phone calls, coming from the very top, reduced the number of complaints.

Edgar Williams was buried without fuss or much ceremony. His funeral was sparsely attended because he had few living relatives. His son and his successor at the school were there, however. Afterwards, Muriel settled down to the quiet life that, without thinking about it, she had always known would be her fate. It was neither pleasant nor unpleasant; it was existence.

About a year into her widowhood, the quiet tenor of her life was interrupted by the arrival of a policeman at her door. She could not recall ever having spoken in her life to a policeman before.

'May I come in?' asked the policeman.

Even the most innocent of the innocent believes in these circumstances that a refusal would be tantamount to an admission of guilt.

'Of course,' said Muriel, and offered him a chair in her small sitting room, into which he fitted as comfortably as an elephant in a match-box.

'There's no cause for alarm,' he said, adjusting himself in the chair.

'Can I get you a cup of tea?' asked Muriel.

'That's very kind of you,' said the policeman, as if rejecting a bribe, 'but I've come to take a statement.'

'A statement? What on earth about?'

Muriel had done nothing and witnessed nothing that could interest the police.

'We're making preliminary investigations into certain events – alleged events at this stage – at Freshfields District Hospital.'

'That's where my husband was. But events? What events?'

'I'm not at liberty at this stage to say,' said the policeman. 'At this stage we are only taking statements.'

The policeman asked Muriel to cast her mind back to the day when Edgar (as he called him) was taken to hospital. He wrote her answer down, having put it into his own words, and then, having got her to acknowledge that if she had said anything that she knew to be false she would be liable to prosecution, put it before her to sign, which she did. He asked her whether, if she were called, she would be willing to come to court.

Muriel said that she had never been to court.

'At this stage,' said the policeman, 'there's nothing to worry about.'

The policeman seemed unaware that this implied there might be something to worry about later on.

Two weeks later a policewoman appeared at Muriel's door.

'Hello, Muriel,' she said, with a bright smile. 'I'm your Victim Support Liaison Officer, V.S.L.O. for short.'

'What's that?' asked Muriel.

'A V.S.L.O.?' said the policewoman. 'Well, when someone's been the victim of a serious crime, we support them through the difficult time that follows.'

'Victim of a serious crime? But I haven't been the victim of a serious crime.'

Had she come to the right address? The policewoman looked at a clipboard she had with her.

'You are Muriel Williams, widow of the Mr Edgar Williams?'

'Yes, I am. Why?'

'Well, you have been the victim of a serious crime, or at least may have been.'

'Have I? I never knew.'

'Didn't anyone inform you?' The V.S.L.O. tutted. Typical! Her job was hard enough already. 'We think your husband may have been poisoned.'

Poisoned? Surely they could not have believed what Edgar said. Would she never be free of this absurd idea of his?

'You don't believe…?'

'Believe what?' asked the V.S.L.O..

'That I poisoned him?'

The V.S.L.O. was very professional: no flicker of an expression passed over her face. She patted Muriel on the knee.

'It's good to have made contact,' she said. 'I'll be your V.S.L.O. until the Court Proceeding Liaison Officer takes over, the C.P.L.O. I know it's a bit confusing, all these letters.' She handed Muriel a card. 'There's my telephone number to call me if you need me. You can call me at any time.'

Three days later a young man in a slightly lumpy black suit and with slicked-back hair, stood on Muriel's doorstep.

'I'm Detective Constable Jones,' he said pleasantly as he flicked open a kind of wallet with a picture of himself in it, accompanied by some tiny writing and a signature. Then he flicked it shut again. 'Can I come in?'

Muriel was becoming almost used to strange arrivals and departures. The neighbours must also have noticed.

'Yes, of course,' she replied.

He settled himself into the same armchair as the first policeman had used. She noticed that his shoes were those of a man who was trying to be smart but who had not the taste that came with breeding.

'There's nothing to be worried about at this stage,' he said. 'We're just making routine enquiries.'

'What about?' asked Muriel.

'Your husband died in suspicious circumstances. We have to explore every possibility, as I'm sure you understand. You'd want nothing less, I'm sure.'

Muriel said nothing.

'You're not under oath at this stage.' The detective took out his notebook. 'Did you visit your husband while he was in hospital?' he asked.

'No.'

'Why not?'

'I was waiting for an operation. On my hip.'

'In which hospital?'

'Prester General.'

'Why not Freshfields District?'

'They don't do hips there, that's what I was told.'

'Did you know that your husband would have to go to hospital when you arranged for your operation?'

'I didn't arrange for it. They phoned me just before to tell me.'

'How long before?'

'The night before.'

'Are you sure?'

'Yes. Does it really matter?'

The detective did not reply. Instead, he asked:

'Have you ever set foot in Freshfields District Hospital?'

'No, I've never had any reason to – until my husband was admitted to it, of course, and then there wasn't time. He wasn't there long.'

Her reply had no visible effect on the detective. He continued:

'Did you know which ward your husband would be admitted to?'

'No.'

'Did you know which ward your husband *had been* admitted to?'

'I suppose I must have been told, but I can't remember.'

'Does the name Cesarino Mangopal mean anything to you?'

Muriel could not hide her astonishment. What a strange name, and what a strange question!

'No, should it?' she said.

'It will soon be in the newspapers and on television. He's just been arrested on suspicion of murder.'

'Of my husband?'

'Not exactly. It's come to light that there were a lot of unexpected sudden deaths in Freshfields Hospital, including that of your husband. We think that in some cases they were caused by the administration of insulin. That doesn't necessarily mean that your husband was among them.'

'How many people?'

'We know of at least five cases, but there may have been more. We know of cases where it was tried and failed, that is if the intention was to kill.'

How could such a thing have happened in a hospital with doctors and nurses everywhere? Surely they must have noticed something?

The detective got up to go.

'Your V.S.L.O. will keep you informed of development in the case,' he said. 'She'll call on you again soon.'

Three weeks later, another policewoman called. Once settled in the chair, she said:

'I'm sorry for the misunderstanding, but I'm sure that in a case like this, we have to leave no stone unturned.'

'You thought I poisoned my husband?'

'No, no, of course not. It was just that... it was just that every possibility has to be explored. Murderers sometimes have accomplices.' She smiled. 'Anyway, we're not even sure that Edgar was killed. But Victim Support is here to help you through this difficult period.'

'But surely, if my husband was poisoned, he was the victim.

And if he wasn't…'

The policewoman was ready for this. Old people were all the same, old-fashioned, she'd heard it before. She was ready with her lecture.

'When a crime is committed,' she said, 'it's not just the victim of the crime who's victimised, but everyone around the victim. They are victims too, and the closer they are to the victim, the more victimised they are. We call them secondary victims.'

'But you don't even know whether my husband was poisoned.'

The policewoman was ready for this too.

'Yes, of course. But the mere fact that he was in hospital at the time of the other offences must affect you, even if he wasn't one of the victims. It's just the same as if he was.

Muriel, who didn't like to be rude, remained silent, and the policewoman took her silence to mean that she had understood.

'So I'll be coming to see you from time to time to keep you up to date and check that you're all right.'

But she never came again. Instead, about three months later, another policewoman, this one very tall, arrived on her doorstep.

'I'm your new Victim Liaison Support Officer, or V.S.L.O. for short,' she said lightly. 'My name's Samantha, but everyone calls me Sam.'

'What happened to the other…?'

'To Sharon? She was moved from Victim Liaison Support to Child Abuse Co-ordination. They're putting more resources into Child Abuse since the Burton Report. You must have heard of the Burton Report?'

'I don't think so,' said Muriel.

'You must have, it was all over the papers – you know, after the Church of Flesh case?'

Muriel shook her head.

'I don't remember,' she said.

'Oh, you must. That was the sect that cooked and ate their children as a ritual. It was in the newspapers and on the telly for weeks.'

There were worse things than being poisoned in hospital, then.

'The Burton Report said that members of the Church of Flesh didn't get enough support from the community, so there's been a shift into child abuse. As it happens, Sharon's now on maternity leave, she's going to have a baby. But the shift means we're a bit thin on the ground in Victim Support. That's why we haven't been to see you for so long. Anyway, back to Edward.'

'Edgar,' said Muriel.

'Yes, Edgar, that's right, sorry. I just thought I'd call to let you know how the case's getting on.'

'Thank you, very good of you.'

'Cesarino Mangopal is put down for trial in seven months. We're pretty confident of success.'

'That's nice,' said Muriel.

'You can never be quite sure, of course. But the evidence against him looks pretty strong. Anyway, because the trial date has now been set, it'll be the W.L.S.T., the Witness Liaison and Support Team, that'll be looking after you. I just thought I'd let you know. They're very good. And I've come as well to say goodbye from the Victim Support Liaison Team and to thank you for all your co-operation. We appreciate it a lot.'

'Am I going to be a witness, then?' asked Muriel.

'I'm afraid I can't say. Witness Liaison will let you know for definite. I suppose you will be, or they wouldn't be involved. Of course, it depends on counsel, he decides. I'm not sure any decision has been made yet.'

Samantha – Sam – left, and Muriel never saw her again. However, seven months later Witness Liaison visited her in the shape of a dumpy woman with artificially frisé hair.

'I've got good news for you, Muriel,' she said. 'You're not needed as a witness after all.'

'Why not?'

'The prosecution's decided not to proceed with Edgar's case. The coroner's dragged his feet over the cause of Edgar's death, so we still don't know. As there's no charge against Mangopal in Edgar's case, your evidence wouldn't be admissible. Anyway, there's enough evidence against him in other cases to convict him several times over.'

'I would like to know how Edgar died.'

'Well of course, I can understand that, but even if the coroner finds that he was poisoned, I don't think there'd be a trial.'

'No trial? Why not?'

'It wouldn't be in the public interest. After all, the culprit would already have been found guilty of five counts of murder and sentenced to life imprisonment. What would be the point of trying him again? A man has only one life he can spend in prison.'

'You mean it would all just be forgotten?' asked Muriel.

'Oh no,' replied the woman from Witness Support, 'not at all. It would what we call lie on the file. This means the case against him could be re-opened at any time.'

'But why would anyone do that?'

'Precisely. But suppose Mangopal appealed and was released on a technicality. They could re-arrest him at once and charge him with your husband's murder. If, that is, there were enough evidence against him.'

The woman from Witness Support looked as if she thought she had just proved a difficult geometric theorem. She embarked on an alternative proof.

'Trials are very expensive. Just think of all the organisation and co-ordination involved. You have to get the judge and the barristers and the witnesses all together at the same time. It can be a nightmare...'

'Yes,' said Muriel. 'Terrible.'

'So you see, it's not the kind of thing you would do unless it was absolutely necessary in the public interest, especially with all these budget cuts.'

The woman from Witness Support stood up to leave.

'I must be going,' she said, looking at her watch. 'I'm glad to have cleared up any misunderstanding. But ring me if you have any other questions.'

She left Muriel a card.

After a further delay of three months, the trial of Cesarino

Mangopal went ahead. It emerged that his nursing certificate was a forgery, and that he had been expelled from his nursing school for various malpractices, from theft to illicit sex. His glowing testimonials were from people who had never existed, or had been dead at the time, or who did not write them. Under cross-examination, the Director of Nursing Practice and Development of Freshfields District Hospital said that it had been better to have Mangopal than nobody at all, and that in any case he had given no reason for dissatisfaction with his work.

Throughout the trial the accused remained absolutely impassive. His face was mask-like, betraying neither emotion nor thought. This was attributed by some of the less intellectual newspapers to his part-Chinese ancestry. There was not even a flicker of recognition at the names of his alleged victims. This, naturally, went to prove how guilty he was: an innocent man would have reacted.

Cesarino Mangopal had killed at random. He had no particular reason to kill the people he did kill; he had nothing individual against them and no connection with them. The lack of obvious motive had made detection difficult, as had the cunning of his method. The evidence against him was purely circumstantial, but that is often the best kind of evidence. No one had seen him do anything. If only he hadn't kept a secret diary, he might never have been caught.

He had put insulin into infusion bags without knowing to whom they would subsequently be given and was not personally present when they had their effect on patients. When he learnt of an unexpected death on the ward, he expressed neither surprise, nor sorrow, nor even triumph. He was not a man to give himself away.

Once he had been found guilty, the newspapers and television speculated on his motives, which had not emerged at trial. Psychologists speculated fluently. It was obvious to some that Mangopal had killed because of resentment at being passed over for promotion in favour of a Ghanaian woman, even though, with a forged certificate, he was not entitled to a job in the first place. Others said that he had a subtle form of brain damage that prevented him from feeling any empathy with others and whom he therefore thought of as mere objects, and inconvenient and demanding ones at that. He derived no monetary gain from his activities, which would at least have rendered them easily comprehensible. Of course, the fact that his mother died early in his life did not help. Probably he resented the survival of people beyond the age at which his mother died. Why should they survive when his mother hadn't?

The woman from Witness Support called on Muriel once more after Mangopal was convicted and sentenced to life imprisonment with the recommendation that he remain in prison for fourteen years. She was almost exultant at the excellent news.

'What about my husband?' asked Muriel. 'Did Mangopal kill him?'

'It's impossible to be certain with a trial,' said the woman. 'I spoke to one of the detectives in the case though I'm not supposed to. He told me that we will probably never know. It's too late for exhumation. But it doesn't really matter, does it? I mean, even if he did do it, well… he's in for a long time. He won't do it again in a hurry!'

The woman from Witness Support had been sitting in Edgar's chair.

If only Muriel had not agreed to her operation, which after all was not life-saving, Edgar might still be sitting in it.

II

PANACEA

LOWHAMPTON WAS A TOWN in decline from a level that had never been very high. First the kitchenware factory that employed a quarter of the population migrated to the other side of the world; then they built both a ring road and a by-pass, the former acting as a mediaeval moat to keep people out and the latter ensuring that the town was no longer on the way to anywhere. No one would now break his journey to visit it, not even its sixteenth century half-timbered inn, the Sun and Bear, with its arrays of fruit machines and wide-screen televisions re-laying football matches, live and recorded, from all over Europe. Only the worst young people stayed behind: those who wore hoodies and sold cannabis or amphetamines on street corners.

R. N. Smith (Established 1975) was a hardware store in the high street, situated between a boarded-up pizza parlour that had gone bankrupt from too much competition and a charity shop for abandoned reptiles that sold everything from airport paperback novels with garish covers to shiny china dogs and moth-eaten fox-fur stoles, the glass eyes of whose heads were missing.

R. N. Smith (Established 1975), proprietor R. N. Smith, was not flourishing. Either people didn't bother to repair or replace anything for themselves any more, or they went elsewhere, to the large do-it-yourself emporium on the other side of the ring-road which sold things at discounted prices. According to R. N., this was false economy, for it would lead to monopoly and then to price-hikes.

The proprietor himself, as his wife and assistant always referred to him on the phone, had not moved with the times. He maintained that computers were a passing fashion, compared with card indexes and a leather-bound sale ledger. He was too young to retire and too old to change. Sales had risen in inverse proportion to expenses. R. N., as his wife called him in the intimacy of their home, was lucky even to break even. Fortunately, he had paid off his mortgage.

R. N. was a man of principle. Do screws change, he had asked his brother-in-law when the letter suggested varying his stock? Besides, with trade so precarious, this was not the time to take risks. He therefore continued to wear the chocolate-brown coat with white buttons secured by wire that he had worn from the day that he had opened the shop all those years ago. If it were not the same actual coat, it was at least identical in appearance. It gave the world a little much-needed stability.

Mrs Smith, who 'did the books', was fully aware of the situation but never mentioned it. They talked of anything but the situation, and one might have thought, listening to them, that the future of the world was of more importance to them than the future of their business. Each of them knew, however, what the other was thinking: that disaster was just round the corner.

One evening, after the meal they called tea (Mrs Smith was what she called a good plain cook, which is to say that she could remove the flavour from anything), R. N. settled to read the only newspaper that entered their house, the weekly *Lowhampton Gazette* (incorporating the Frampton-on-Avon Mercury). It was not an exciting publication, for the small change of life in Lowhampton could hardly have been smaller, except when a drug-addicted lout broke into an old lady's house and bludgeoned her to death while stealing her microwave oven. On this occasion, however, it had headlines half an inch tall:

VAST NEW PROJECT FOR TOWN

The Gazette's sole reporter, a man who always wore a tie but seldom did up the top button of his shirt, and most of whose research was conducted in the pub, for once conveyed some enthusiasm and even excitement:

> Lowhampton secured a huge victory last week in being selected as the site of the new National Hospital for Occult Diseases against fierce competition from other towns. The nation has expressed its confidence in Lowhampton. Work on the project will start immediately and the project is expected to cost in excess of £2 billion. A new era has dawned for Lowhampton!

The reporter then displayed the extent of his classical learning, that obviously emerged after the consumption of several pints, by adding at the bottom of the article the words *Fiat lux!*

R. N. showed the article to his wife, Frieda. He said that the population and importance of the town would increase, and so would sales.

'And shop rents,' said Frieda.

'You always look on the gloomy side,' said R. N. – as, of course, did he.

'And haven't I always been proved right?'

'This time it's different.'

'We'll see.'

The bulldozers moved in soon afterwards. They were larger than some of the small houses of the back streets of Lowhampton, which were pushed aside and almost instantly reduced to rubble. Before long a vast field of mud sown with loose bricks had been produced, as after a battle during the Great War. The trees had gone with the houses, and the field seemed to stretch as far as the eye could see.

Then huge holes were dug in the ground by machines with wheels as tall as the elephants in Hannibal's army. The men who controlled them by comparison were like the little birds that perch on great animals, picking the insect parasites off their skin. A forest of steel pillars grew up from the ground and then the skeleton of a building. Nothing remained the same from day to day, and before long the skeleton was covered in glossy stone cladding. The windows were narrow, fortress-like slits in the façade, with dark smoked glass.

Before long, the building was larger than the rest of the town put together, or so it seemed. It was eleven storeys high, and from the sixth storey you would have been able to see the sprawl of Lowhampton far beneath. From the town itself, the hospital resembled a tsunami about to engulf it and sweep it away like so much matchwood.

The Gazette was exultant:

NATIONAL HOSPITAL COMPLETED IN RECORD TIME

From the reporter's account, you might have supposed that it was the skill and industry of the people of the town that was responsible for this triumph: but no one from the town had been employed in the construction. The workers were strangers to the town, accommodated in tents and containers beyond the site itself.

'It's marvellous how quick they've done it,' said Frieda, looking at the picture in the *Gazette*. Actually, you didn't have to look in the *Gazette* to see it: the hospital was inescapable from wherever in the town you looked. You sensed it there even with your back turned.

'It hasn't brought any business,' said R. N..

'Just as I always said it wouldn't,' said Frieda.

'It's because it hasn't opened yet,' said R.N.. 'The builders are just here to get the job done. You wait till it opens. There'll be all the doctors and nurses living in the town. They'll need things.'

R. N. and Frieda had sometimes wondered what Occult Diseases could be, but since they got no further than that they could have nothing to do with the Occult – black magic or levitation – they ceased to wonder.

The day of the grand opening arrived, but not even the Mayor of Lowhampton – Councillor Mrs Bayes, wife of the local butcher who was suspected of putting sawdust in his sausages –

was invited. No one from the town was of sufficient importance to attend the opening of a national institution that would, it was asserted in one of the opening speeches, be World Class. The Minister himself came, accompanied by the husband of a cousin of the Queen, decked out in a splendid uniform, who actually cut the ribbon with the gold, or at least gilded, scissors. The applause that greeted this heroic act after the Minister had made a speech that no one beyond the front row could hear because the public address system failed, but the text of which nevertheless appeared in the next edition of the *Gazette*, died out in the open air as if extinguished by invisible sprinklers. Then the husband of the Queen's cousin and the Minister were lifted out by helicopter, while the rest of the guests left in black limousines.

After the hospital's opening, Lowhampton seemed even quieter and more depressed than ever. To ordinary torpor was added anti-climax. There were fewer people in the streets and even the unemployed youths in baseball caps turned backwards or sideways disappeared.

About two weeks after the grand opening, Frieda, at the end of the day when R. N. had not served a single customer, told him that their neighbour, a woman who was always trying to engage others in footling conversation, had been taken to the new hospital in an ambulance that morning. R. N. was not interested in their neighbour, but felt that he had to say something.

'What was wrong with her?'

'How do I know?' replied Frieda. 'She seemed perfectly well yesterday when she told me her son had failed his accountancy exams again. I wasn't surprised. He never worked very hard and wasn't very bright to begin with.'

R. N. grunted, not without satisfaction. The failure of others always pleased him.

'Anyway,' said Frieda, 'you should've seen her go.'

'Why?'

'The ambulance came with four motorbikes round it with flashing lights.'

'Must've been an emergency.'

'I don't think so.'

'Waste of money, then. No wonder the country's in the mess it's in. They wouldn't do it with their own money.'

There was a lull in the conversation as if the matter was closed or exhausted. Put out by his uninterest in what she had to say, his wife asked:

'Aren't you going to ask me why?'

'Why what?'

'Why they sent four police motorbikes with the ambulance.'

'Why did they?'

'They came just in case she wouldn't agree to go,' said Frieda, with the triumph of one party to secret information.

'Why wouldn't she agree to go?' asked R. N.. 'After all, she must have called the ambulance in the first place.'

'That's just it. She didn't, it just arrived for her.'

'Her husband must've called it for her, then.'

'He didn't.'

'How do you know?'

'I asked him. They dragged her from the front door to the ambulance.'

'Well, someone must've called it.'

R. N. opened an old copy of the *Gazette* to put an end to the conversation. After all these years together, his wife had never really understood that what he wanted – needed – after a day doing nothing much in the shop, which was tiring in its own way, was silence. On the other hand, he had never really understood that what she wanted – needed – after a day at home was to talk.

'She screamed,' said Frieda, as R.N. read an account of how Lowhampton Wanderers had been relegated to the third division of the local league.

'Who screamed?' asked R. N. distractedly.

'She did, of course. Who else are we talking about? Take an interest.'

'Why did she scream?'

'Because she was being dragged away, because she didn't want to go.'

'Why not?'

'I don't know. Perhaps she thought there was nothing wrong with her.'

'There must've been. Why else would they have come for her?'

And there the matter rested for lack of further information. R. N. was not a man with a speculative turn of mind.

Five days later, however, his wife informed him on his return from the shop that the ambulance had come this time for her husband, though he had gone quietly, without making a fuss.

'He must've caught something off his wife,' said R. N..

'He was perfectly all right yesterday,' she said. 'He was out in the garden.'

'We don't know, we can't say, we're not doctors,' said R. N.. 'Perhaps he has something going on inside.'

Something going on inside could not be good.

'Well, funny, I call it.'

'Anyway, it's none of our business.'

Four days later, however, it was R. N.'s turn to announce some news.

'An ambulance came today to Reptile Rescue and took Mrs Greel and Miss Finch away.' They were the old ladies who served in the shop as volunteers. They thought they were doing good because Reptile Rescue was a charity.

'There must be something going round,' said Frieda. 'A virus or something.'

It was true that Lowhampton was susceptible to epidemics. Last winter everyone had had a cold.

'I hope we don't catch it, whatever it might be,' said R. N. 'We can't afford not to open.'

The *Gazette* was out that day, and R. N. read the headline:

MYSTERY ILLNESS: WANDERERS' GAME CANCELLED

Apparently the goalkeeper and the centre-half had been admitted to hospital, and so had the reserves who played in their positions. This was surprising because they were fit young men, if a little overweight from drinking after the game.

'Something's going on,' said R. N. gnomically, but then he put it from his mind. There was enough to worry about without concerning oneself with things that did not concern one.

But a week later, a strange letter arrived, addressed to Frieda. On the envelope, in large scarlet lettering, was the word OF-FICIAL. Then, in black lettering of equal size, were the words, IMPORTANT INFORMATON ABOUT YOUR HEALTH. OPEN IMMEDIATELY. DO NOT IGNORE.

'What can it be?' asked Frieda. 'I feel perfectly all right.'

'How do I know?' asked R.N. 'Open it and see.'

She tore it open and unfolded the page inside. It was addressed from the National Hospital for Occult Diseases, with a mission statement in flowing font: Halting the progression of disease. There was a bar code on the top right-hand corner of the page.

Although it bore her name and address and even her date of birth, the letter did not address her directly. She read it out to R. N.:

> Our review of your medical records showed that you may be suffering from a serious occult disease. This is a risk not only to yourself but to those around you, your family and the community. It is therefore essential for you, your family and the community that you should be investigated medically as thoroughly as possible.

Frieda, who was not used to reading aloud, paused.

'An occult disease? What's that?' she asked.

'It's hidden,' said R.N. 'You don't know you've got it. Diseases have to start some time, I suppose. They creep up on you before you know you've got them. These days they can detect them with scans and things.'

'What things?'

'Blood tests and the like.'

'And how do they have my records? I never gave them no permission.'

'These days they're all on computer,' said R.N.. R.N. still didn't believe in computers: what if there was a power cut? 'They have only to press a button to get them, creepy I call it. But there's nothing to worry about: they must know what they're doing.'

She resumed her reading out loud:

Doctors have reviewed your case records and determined that you require urgent admission to the hospital. No firm date can yet be given for this, but it will be at some time within the next two weeks and you should hold yourself in readiness. An ambulance will call for you as soon as a bed has become available. For the moment there is no need for you to do anything except have a bag of nightclothes and toiletries at the ready. Please note that this should not exceed 7 (seven) kilos in weight or be larger in size than 35 (thirty-five) centimetres by 35 (thirty-five) centimetres by 25 (twenty-five) centimetres. Please note that the hospital does not accept any responsibility for the safety or loss of your possessions while you are in the hospital.

'The cheek of it!' said Frieda.

'They're only trying to cover their backs,' said R. N..

Frieda resumed:

Admission to the hospital is for your own benefit and for the safety of those around you. Please bring this letter with you to facilitate your admission.

At the foot of the letter, in large bold lettering were the words:

WARNING
Failure to cooperate may result in a fine of up to £5000

'I'm not going,' said Frieda, with a sudden jut of her jaw.

'They can't make me.'

'It's for your own good,' said R.N.. 'And we can't afford to pay £5000.'

'Well, we'll see.'

'Yes, we'll see,' said R. N..

Later that evening, Frieda packed a small bag of things 'just in case' and because 'you never knew'. And from then on, try as she might not to do so, she found herself listening out for the arrival of the ambulance. And since the traffic in the road seemed to have dwindled since the opening of the hospital, it would be all the easier to hear its arrival.

R. N. continued his work as usual, though trade, like the traffic, had dwindled. The staff at the huge hospital must have been very numerous and probably well-paid: but they were never seen in the town, and never needed what R. N. sold. They had their town apart, like a camp in Saudi Arabia. Every day, before he left for work, R. N. told Frieda to call him at the shop if the ambulance came for her. To what purpose, he did not say, and did not know himself.

Nothing happened for several days, except that there was a slight increase in tension as the two-week deadline approached. Then, one evening, R. N. returned home to find the house empty: the ambulance had come for Frieda. He was mildly irritated that she had not followed his instruction to call him, but in truth there had not been time enough for her to do so. The ambulance crew had been in a terrible hurry and said that they had many people to fetch before the end of the day. They had been dressed in the kind of white overalls that those who disinter bodies of the disappeared from dustbins and shallow illicit graves wear, and they had been flanked by two policemen dressed all in black, and who had rapped imperiously on the front door. Handcuffs dangled conspicuously from their belts. They also carried cannisters with which to spray people.

'Mrs Frieda Smith?' asked one of the ambulance men stepping forward as she opened the door, his voice muffled by the surgical mask he was wearing.

'Yes?' said Frieda, who tried to make her answer as much a

question as possible.

'It's time. You received your letter, I presume.'

'Yes,' said Frieda.

'Bring your bag, please.' He knew she had packed one, because they all had. For their reluctance, they obeyed. And his
'please' was an order.

'I want to phone my husband.'

'There's no time for that, I'm afraid. And please don't bring
any mobile phones, tablets or laptops with you, they may interfere with our systems in the hospital.'

The two policemen stiffened, as if expecting to meet resistance, but Frieda offered none. Fortunately her packed bag was
near to hand and on brief inspection was found to be within the
regulation size and weight, so there was no delay on its account.
But as she stepped from her front door, the two ambulance men
gripped her firmly just above the elbow to guide her into the
waiting vehicle, which was marked *National Hospital for Occult
Diseases: Transforming Prevention into Cure* on its side. There
were three other words in a line underneath: *Caring for Everyone.*

The inside of the ambulance was very different from how
Frieda had imagined it. There were no stretchers, no bottles
of oxygen, no screens with green lines going up and down on
them emitting bleeps from time to time. It was more like a comfortable living room with four armchairs round a coffee table.
The ambulance men told her to sit in the one of her choice and
do up her seatbelt, whereupon a pre-recorded message emerged
from an invisible speaker, and suffused the interior like a gas.
'For your comfort and safety, please keep your seatbelt fastened
at all times until the ambulance has come to a full and final
stop. For monitoring purposes, and to improve our service,
your journey will be recorded on CCTV.' These days walls had
not only ears, but eyes.

The journey was short, since nowhere in Lowhampton was
far from the hospital. The empty streets flashed past through
the smoked windows, and the ambulance drew up under an
enormous modern *porte cochère* of glass and steel. The doors of

the ambulance opened automatically, and a recorded woman's voice said 'Please alight taking all of your belongings with you, as these cannot be returned to you once you have left the vehicle. And please mind the step as you alight.'

The ambulance men signalled where she should go, which direction she should take, though it was obvious in any case. Two huge glass doors slid noiselessly open as she approached them and once inside she seemed to be trapped inside a glass chamber, for there were two more doors before her that did not open immediately after the first two doors closed behind her. Two cameras above her moved like insects' antennae. Was she being inspected or disinfected, or both? After a few moments, however, the doors in front of her slid open and a message, Welcome to the National Hospital for Occult Diseases was relayed from nowhere and everywhere.

Frieda was now in a vast atrium. She was greeted by two women in blindingly white tunics. 'Welcome to the National Hospital for Occult Disease,' one of them said. 'First you have to register,' said the other.

They escorted her to a counter made of glass. There sat another woman in a white tunic. She told Frieda to look straight into a little camera perched on the counter that seemed almost alive, and then to put her right forefinger on a pad.

When Frieda had done so, the woman behind the counter looked at a hidden computer screen before her and read out what she called Frieda's 'details': her name, address, date of birth, husband's and doctor's name, bank, and parents' date of death.

'Is that correct?' she asked.

'Yes,' said Frieda. 'How do you know all that?'

'Biometrics,' said the woman. 'You have a longevity index of 0.21.'

'What's that?' asked Frieda.

'Your chance of living to the normal age of ninety-five is twenty-one per cent, which is very low. That's why you're being admitted.'

'Come with us,' said one of the two women who had greeted her. 'We'll show you to your room.'

She followed them, hardly noticing anything except shininess everywhere. Everything was bright and smooth, easily wiped down. Frieda, a conscientious housewife, noticed that.

Her room was on the seventh floor. By the time she reached it, she would had no idea how to return whence she had come. Doors in the hospital never had to be pushed or pulled open: they always slid. Some opened seemingly of their own volition, others only in response to a tag which each of the two women possessed. Frieda felt small, unimportant, by comparison with those who had the electronic keys to the doors.

Finally they reached what they told her was her room. It was large and comfortable, in the manner of a good airport hotel. The narrow window, that extended the length of one wall, was of tinted glass to prevent the glare of the sun, if any, but it could not be opened. Frieda asked about opening the window, but was told that it was impossible: there was no need to open it, or rather there was a need not to open it, since the air in the room, and indeed the whole hospital, was carefully monitored and controlled, for example for carbon dioxide content. Air from outside would upset the equilibrium control. The same went for temperature, which was kept both invariable and optimal. Sound no more than air reached the room from the outside world; it was as if it were absorbed at once by some kind of blotting paper for noise. Light from outside, never very bright, could be excluded altogether by electrically-operated shutters.

On the wall opposite the bed was affixed a large screen:

WELCOME MRS R. N. SMITH
SCROLL DOWN FOR MENU

One of the women in a white tunic showed her how. She could select the food she wanted and the films or sport she wanted to watch. News was not available.

'Research has shown that news increases heart rate and anxiety,' one of the two women said.

'I ought to phone my husband,' said Frieda.

'That's not allowed,' said one of the two women. 'We need to monitor you for a time free of all outside influences that could affect or disturb your physiology. We want to get to know the real you.'

'When will I be able to speak to him, then?'

'That depends on how quickly you settle down to a state of equilibrium. Remote contacts postpone it unnecessarily.'

'We need to increase your Longevity Index first,' said the other woman. 'In the meantime, you'll be very comfortable.'

They showed Frieda a nightdress and dressing gown to be worn at all times in the hospital. Clean ones would be delivered every day.

'We'll leave you now,' one of them said. 'The Professor will come soon to make his preliminary assessment.'

'His preliminary assessment?' asked Frieda. 'What's that?'

'Of the interventions that you need to raise your Longevity Index.'

The two women departed. The door slid shut behind them and she was on her own in a silence that seemed almost dense. It disturbed her: she had never heard anything like it before. She listened intently, but no sound came. She tried to bring something upon on the screen to break the eeriness of it, but a message came up:

NO ENTERTAINMENT AVAILABLE UNTIL
PRELIMINARY ASSESSMENT COMPLETED

There was nothing for it but to sit in the armchair and await what was to happen next.

Fortunately, she had not long to wait. Another message flashed on the screen:

PROFESSOR APPROACHING!
PROFESSOR APPROACHING!

The door slid open and a tall, athletic, elegant, suntanned and handsome man with whose ice-blue eyes that never reveal what is going on behind them stepped into the room. The door slid shut after him.

'Good morning,' he said. 'I am the Professor.' There was a label on the lapel of his white coat but Frieda could not make out the name. 'Welcome to the National Hospital. We will do everything possible to make your stay comfortable. So comfortable, in fact, that you won't want to leave!' He smiled, revealing iceberg teeth.

'Thank you,' said Frieda. 'But I don't really understand why I am here. I feel perfectly all right.'

'Ah, many of our patients say that,' said the Professor. 'At least at first. But of course, health is more than a mere matter of absence of disease or of symptoms, as I am sure you are aware.'

'What do you mean?'

'Modern illness is not as it was a century ago,' said the Professor. 'A century ago, illness struck suddenly, or so it appeared, without warning. I am sure you know the passage from Donne: 'This minute I was well, and am ill this minute.' But things are not like that any more. These days illness starts stealthily, without the sufferer even knowing that anything is wrong. He carries the risk within him like a time bomb, as it were, sometimes for decades in advance. We at the National Hospital aim to defuse the time bomb, so to speak, that all of us carry within us.'

'But if we all...' began Frieda.

'Yes, I know what you are going to say,' interrupted the Professor, who had heard it all before. 'But the fact is that the time bombs within us are all timed to go off at different times. Some will go off in a week's time, and some in twenty, thirty or even fifty years.'

'Then how do you...?'

The Professor laughed.

'It's all a matter of probabilities,' he said. 'We work it out by using a large number of variables: the larger the number, the greater the accuracy. For example, we know in your case that you have a forty-eight per cent chance of dying between the age of seventy and seventy-five. This itself is at least seventy-six per cent higher than it should be, or need be, compared with the average or median of your age. That is a terrible injustice which we aim to correct.'

Frieda nodded, not because she understood, but because it seemed to be expected of her.

'Why should you die before others, and before it is necessary? What have you done to deserve it, other than having lived an unhealthy life through ignorance? And in any case, why should the average or the median be your yardstick rather than the possible? Why not take the person who lives to be a hundred and five as your model? Is it not fundamentally unjust that some people live longer than others, as much as by thirty years, if we exclude cases of exceptionally early demise? We at the National Hospital are dedicated to rooting out this injustice once and for all. We want everyone to die at the same age, as old as possible.'

Frieda looked at him uncomprehendingly.

'How long will I be here?' she asked.

'As short a time as possible,' replied the Professor smoothly. 'Until such time as you have reached your target, which is a risk of death at the age of ninety that is fifty per cent below the current average. That is the figure we have promised the government to reach. Of course, it will take time. Our methods aren't perfect yet, though they are improving all the time. We can't know in advance how long it will take to reduce some of your risk factors in the desired direction by the required amount.'

'What do you mean?'

'Well, take your weight as an example,' said the Professor genially. 'According to our calculations, it is three point two kilos too high. This means you have to lose it.'

'I've been trying, but...'

'I'm afraid effort doesn't count. Nature doesn't reward effort, she rewards results. It's what you actually weigh that counts, not what you tried to weigh.'

'It's not fair.'

'That depends on how you look at it. We know that with the right techniques and with sufficient determination everyone can reach his correct weight. Of course, I am not saying that it is easy; if it were easy there would be no need for this hospital.' He laughed. 'Unfortunately, there is no reason why what is necessary should be easy. Nature doesn't make things easy and doesn't consult our convenience. But to return to the question you asked.'

'What question?'

'How long will you be here? I was just pointing out how difficult it would be to predict with any accuracy and I don't want to mislead you. I was trying to illustrate why I cannot fix a time by using your weight as an example. As I said, you have to lose three point two kilos, but how easy that is and how long it takes to do so varies from person to person and is dependent on many variables. For example, there is your metabolic rate. If you metabolise quickly, of course, you lose weight quickly – relatively quickly, that is, compared to people with slow metabolic rates. And your metabolic rate itself is not something inscribed on tablets of stone, it too is dependent on many variables which we have not yet measured.'

Frieda said nothing.

'And that is not the end of the matter, far from it. 'Once you have reached your optimum rate, you have to maintain it, and that is a very complicated and complex matter. There is no point in reaching your optimum weight if you depart from it straight afterwards. In fact, that is what happens to most people if they are left to their own devices because they put on weight easier than they maintain it level, let alone lose it. And there is compelling evidence that losing weight and putting it on again is itself harmful to health, independently of all other considerations. Moreover, it's not healthy to be underweight either. Everyone has only one optimum weight, and one of our most difficult tasks is to make sure that everyone keeps to it long-term. Of course, as you know, it varies slightly with age. That is an added complication. Our methods are still a little experimental.'

'Experimental?' Frieda looked alarmed. Her ideas of experiments were derived from Frankenstein films.

'Oh, there's nothing at all to worry about,' said the Professor. 'We already know the main outlines of treatment, but it remains to refine it slightly, the fine-tuning as it were. As a world-class international centre of excellence in research and development, we are perfectionists. We are searching for perfection – for your benefit, of course.'

Frieda was silent once more.

'We're improving our protocols all the time,' said the Professor.

'Protocols?'

'Yes,' he said. 'These are the pathways, rules if you like, according to which we treat people. Once upon a time, not that long ago, doctors treated patients according to their prejudices or personal experience, or what they had been taught and learnt by rote. It was completely unscientific: medical practice was more like a kind of glorified gossip than a true science. Those days are over, thank goodness. Nowadays, we treat strictly according to the evidence – where it exists, of course. We don't know everything. We'll never know everything, which is why more research will always be necessary, and you are helping us in it. We are getting there slowly, bit by bit. Nature is yielding her secrets. In the meantime, we continue to treat people according to the very best evidence available, while we search for even better evidence. You're helping us find it by being here, so that in the future people will not suffer what you suffer from.'

'But I feel all right.'

'I know that but, as I've tried to explain to you, feeling all right and being all right are not at all the same thing. You have a much higher chance of dying prematurely than you ought, or need, to have.'

'Dying of what?'

'Both of specific causes and of all causes. Specific causes are things like heart attack or stroke, or cancer, that is to say a named disease. All causes means what it says, that is to say the aggregate of all causes of death, from sarcoidosis to suicide. Thus we can know that you are more likely to die of something than others of your age, but we cannot say exactly of what.'

'Then how...?'

'How can we prevent your death?' The Professor laughed again. 'That's simple: even if we don't know what you're going to die of, we know the risk factors that will lead to your death. If we address those risk factors, we prolong your life.'

'How long will it take?'

The Professor smiled.

'Health,' he said, 'is the work of a lifetime. It is a process rather than a state. It is a matter of habit rather than of moment-to-moment conduct.'

'How do you know when...?'

'There are two separate matters. The first is measuring your risk factors. We already know some of them but not all of them. That is one of the reasons you are here. The second is reducing them and ensuring that they remain reduced.'

'So I need tests?'

'Yes, but probably not in the way you think. We don't need to take blood any more, and no more than two or three scans. There are automatic sensors in this room that tell us most of what we need to know.'

'Sensors?'

'Yes, advanced electronic instruments that tell your heart rate and oxygen saturation and metabolic rate without anything being attached to you. We can record everything about your breathing, for example. That is one of the advantages of having a completely controlled air-flow.'

'But where are they?'

'The sensors?' The Professor laughed again. 'You don't need to know that. We don't want anyone interfering with them, do we? They would be very expensive to replace or even repair. But in fact they are very tiny, you can hardly see them. Even I don't know exactly where they are, whether in the ceiling, walls, or bed, depending on what they are measuring. The results are fed into a computer so that your progress can be constantly monitored. Everything's confidential, of course. Only authorised staff has access to the computer.'

Frieda had a vague feeling that her questions had not been fully answered, but she was not used to prolonged discussion and the Professor spoke with complete assurance and authority.

'So,' he continued, 'all you have to do, as they say in airliners, is sit back, relax and enjoy your stay with us. We are here for your comfort and safety.' He paused. 'Any further questions?'

Frieda had many question marks in her mind, but no questions.

'No,' she said.

'Good,' said the Professor. 'Everything is clear.'

He slid open the door with his electronic key. Frieda was alone again.

She looked around her. She went to the window. She could see Lowhampton below, with two cars crawling through it silently. Somehow it looked very unreal, as if it did not concern her in the least. Reality was now the interior of her room.

There was nothing for it but to turn the television on. Without prompting, it demanded that she choose the salad for her next meal. With or without quinoa? She decided with, out of curiosity: she did not know what it was (R. N. would have refused it on the same grounds). She resolved to enjoy whatever there was to enjoy.

When R. N. returned home from work that day and found his wife gone from the house, he knew at once what had happened to her, as it had by then happened to so many others. After a cup of tea, which he made himself, he tried to find out exactly where she was in the hospital so that he could visit her.

This turned out to be not a simple matter. He had no telephone number for the hospital and neither did anyone else. Directory enquiries even denied knowledge of the hospital's existence. In vain did R. N. protest that they must have the number because the hospital was huge and he could see it from his window.

But the voice on the other end of the line was unconnected to human larynx and sounded as if it was submerged under water.

'I'm sorry, I didn't catch that. Can you repeat it?'

It was only a machine, and it was absurd to obey it, but R. N. did so.

'I'm sorry, I still didn't catch your question. Thank you for calling. Goodbye.'

R. N. didn't hold with the internet, but on this occasion was obliged to make use of it. A strange message came up on the screen:

FOR MEDICAL REASONS, THIS COMPUTER HAS BEEN DISABLED. DO NOT TRY TO SWITCH IT ON.

For medical reasons? What could they be? It was absurd. It was... R. N. couldn't think of the words to express the swirl of outrage in his mind. The words then disappeared from the screen and showed a series of pictures of the national Hospital: a smiling nurse with her hand on the shoulder of an equally smiling patient, a laboratory full of shiny electronic equipment, a Japanese garden somewhere deep in the bowels of the building, a patient waving as she was slid into a vast metal tube for a scan of some description, and a group photograph of the staff waving happily to whoever looked at the screen. When the pictures were over, the screen went blank.

R. N. angrily slammed the laptop shut. A fat lot of use it was! He would have to go in person to the hospital. Modern technology indeed!

He walked towards the huge building that loomed so completely over the whole town. You didn't need directions to reach it, only a pair of eyes. It took him about ten minutes to reach the perimeter of the grounds. There was a lawn that had obviously been laid not long before and had had no time to establish itself, and some young trees planted in it, awkward as adolescents in grown-up company. Around the whole was a fence of steel posts strong enough to resist tank attack, strung with razor wire.

R. N. found the entrance. It consisted of two giant sliding gates. There was a kind of guardhouse by one of the gates; through its windows you could see an array of T.V. monitors. Cameras obviously swept every inch of the perimeter and beyond for intruders or escapees. This was absurd: R. N. had sold wire-cutters for years, and none could have dealt with the fence.

Behind a hatch window sat a man in a blue shirt, with the initials NHOD embroidered on it in yellow.

The hatch opened above R. N.'s head. How then was he to

draw attention to his presence? He felt like a diner in a restaurant where the waiter studiously ignores him. The man behind the hatch window must have known that he was there: how else could he have failed to see him for so long? But eventually, slowly, he opened the hatch and looked down at R. N..

'Yes?' he said. He seemed to resent the interruption to whatever he had been doing.

'I've come to visit my wife,' said R. N. 'I think she was brought here today.'

'You think or you know?'

'I think. I mean, it's happened to other people in the town.'

'What has?'

'An ambulance brought them here.'

'Of course it does. This is a hospital. What else would you expect?'

'Well, if my wife, is here, I want to visit her.'

'Name?'

R. N. told him and he looked at a screen, hidden from R. N.'s view.

'Yes, she's here.'

'I want to visit her, then.'

'Do you have a Visitor's Order?'

'What's that?'

'A Visitor's Order?' Did he really have to explain everything? 'It's a signed pass giving you permission to visit. Do you have one?'

'No.'

'I'm not surprised. They usually don't give one for the first three months.'

The hospital hadn't been open that long.

'Why not?'

'Listen mate, I'm not a doctor. How do I know. I'm only the man at the gate.'

'What do I do, then?'

'If I was you, I'd go home and rest. There ain't nothing else for you to do.'

The man closed the hatch.

R. N. turned round and left. He walked home.

He had not long to wait to gain entrance to the hospital. Two days later, during which Frieda had begun to enjoy the luxury of having nothing to do except watch television, R. N. received a letter.

Doctors have reviewed your case records and determined that you require urgent admission to the hospital...

Next day an ambulance called early for him. He was ready for it. His room was identical to Frieda's, but on a different floor.

SMOKESCREEN

THE HISTORY OF THE SECOND English Civil War (which still rages) has yet to be written, and will always be susceptible to revision; but a near-contemporaneous account may be of some use to future historians.

Its origins can be traced to the decision of Sir Filbert Greenweather, the Chief Executive of the Campaign Against Smoking Harms (CASH), to revivify the Campaign. Sir Filbert, because of his many other commitments, worked for it only two afternoons a week, which is why his salary was a mere £150,000; nevertheless, he was genuinely and, as he put it, 'passionately' committed to the cause. For too long, he said, the Campaign had coasted along, contenting itself with tired old educational posters such as the one about the dangers of cigarette ends. There had even been talk of an end to government funding of the Campaign. Something had to be done, and done quickly.

It was at a party that the idea first came to Greenweather. In truth, it was not really his idea at all; but Greenweather had always owed his ascent to the stealthy appropriation of other people's ideas as his own.

He had been speaking at the party to Xavier Fielding, Q.C., the famous advocate who had made his name by defending those accused of terrorism, obscenity or political violence in pursuit of an advanced cause. Fielding was tall and handsome, with flowing grey locks, and his movements had that self-confident liquidity of those who had more than fulfilled their youthful promise. He was tailored with quiet elegance, as befitted a man of his wealth. He had that imperturbable charm that only on reflection gave one pause as to what he was actually thinking. While you were with him, you had the feeling that life was good, or at worst a bit of a joke, and that nothing was to be taken too seriously. To be completely serious, to say anything with only one possible meaning and that could not be taken ironically, even if meant literally, was to be naïve, unsophisticated and, worst of all, a bore. You never quite knew what Xavier Fielding, Q.C., was thinking: he thought in layers.

'We're in a bit of a rut at CASH,' said Greenweather to him (Fielding was one of CASH's trustees). 'It's difficult to know where to go from here. The problem is that everyone already knows how bad smoking is for them. There's a danger of overkill.'

'Death by anti-smoking,' said Fielding, with his smile that never betokened mere amusement.

'Who cares that last year twelve house-fires were caused by smoking in bed?' said Greenweather. 'Most people think it served them right.'

'Yes, that won't fire anyone's imagination,' said Fielding, who always talked for victory, in or out of court.

'We need something new,' said Greenweather.

'How about murder?' said Fielding. 'That's a hardy perennial to capture the public's interest.'

'What do you mean?' asked Greenweather.

'Charge the manufacturers with murder, of having knowingly purveyed fatal products to the public from which hundreds of thousands have died, all for the sake of lucre.'

Greenweather saw at once that it would revive public interest in the cause.

'It might not work,' he said. His first task had always been to think of possible objections.

'Why not?' asked Fielding.

'The Director of Public Prosecutions wouldn't wear it.'

'He might. After all, he prosecutes all manner of innocent people. But it wouldn't matter if he didn't.'

'How so?'

'You could bring a private prosecution.'

A brilliant idea! – but expensive. Even after the recent staff cuts, CASH didn't have a lot of money. Grenweather voiced his doubts.

'We'd represent you pro bono,' said Fielding. 'That's if you can't get a public prosecution, of course.' He lit up one of his famous cigars and drew on it contentedly. Either way, the case would get a lot of attention.

On the way home, the idea grew in Greenweather's mind until it became entirely his own. It wouldn't matter whether or not they won; the newspapers, the television, the social media would be full of it, and publicity was what counted. Greenweather's reputation for dynamism would be enhanced. But he quickly came to the conclusion that a private prosecution would be best, for only in that way could Fielding's services be assured, and he was the only man for the job. His advocacy was famously ferocious, perfectly suited to a case such as this. There was also the factor of time. The law was quite slow enough without the inertia of a government bureaucracy thrown in. Besides, CASH would be only a member of an orchestra in a public prosecution; in a private prosecution, it would be the conductor. No, a private prosecution was best from every possible point of view; a public one would be half-hearted at best, and possibly only *pro forma*. And it would have to be Fielding: Greenweather could tell him that he had failed to interest the public prosecutors, only a small and justified lie. Fielding would be only too pleased to think that vested interest had prevented prosecution: he had made a fortune fighting vested interest. And no one had a good word to say for what Fielding himself had in the past called Big Tobacco. There was nothing Fielding liked more than the role of St George slaying the dragon, or David flinging his fatal stone at Goliath. Even when he lost his battles, his stature as the defender of the little man grew, and in this case therefore he couldn't lose in the wider sense. He would at the very least have brought the law into disrepute as the shield of the rich and powerful: as, in his opinion, it undoubtedly was. Of course, a triumph was also possible.

Greenweather knew his man. Knowledge of his man was another of the reasons for his rise in the world. Fielding would make no difficulties; on the contrary, he would be delighted.

There remained the matter of finances. The case would require scores of witnesses, from professors of epidemiology and respiratory medicine to grieving widows of young victims of diseases caused by smoking. Judges these days were inclined to be sentimental (for fear of public opinion), and there was nothing that swayed them more than a grieving widow, preferably with a child or two thrown in. And then it would be necessary, or at least preferable, to demonstrate that Big Tobacco, or B.T. as Greenweather now thought of it, had known the consequences of smoking all along and had tried to conceal them from the public. Pre-trial publicity and propaganda was also essential, to ensure a properly biased jury.

But the solution to the problem of finances was obvious: Robert Barons, the people's magnate, at least in his own mind. The scion of a rich family, a rebellious failure at school, he had made his first fortune by selling baseball caps to the youth of the poor, but had since branched out into everything from fast food to waste disposal and prisons. He was both militantly casual in his manner and utterly ruthless in his business dealings which, for tax reasons, he conducted mainly from his private island in the Indian Ocean. He was known to be a fierce opponent of smoking, at least of tobacco; he wouldn't allow it on his island or his English estate, though he was much in favour of the legalisation of cannabis, the market in which he hoped to corner when the law changed, and in preparation for which he had established vast plastic greenhouses for the cultivation of tomatoes that could easily be switched to the cultivation of something else.

Sir Filbert thought of him with fastidious distaste, his crocodile smile, his permanent triumphant tan, his assumption of perpetual youth (or adolescence), his smooth but increasingly wrinkled skin, his habit of pawing anyone he met as if he were his intimate, his insidious insinuating friendliness that could turn on a sixpence to enmity the moment a person ceased to be of use to him, but the devil drives where needs must, and perhaps everything could be arranged without personal contact. Barons, who had met him three or four times, would know who Greenweather was; and though Greenweather was not his type (at heart, he had no type, not even toadies), he would decide the matter purely on the basis of his self-interest. Always eager to pose as the friend and companion of the common man, Barons would fund a campaign to have Big Tobacco's directors imprisoned as murderers: it would divert attention from his own tax avoidance.

Barons readily, eagerly agreed. Sitting in his tropical island paradise, nothing gave him greater pleasure than to contemplate the downfall, or even the discomfiture, of the directors of vast but hide-bound companies, besuited and fundamentally nothing but bureaucrats, the kind who had treated him as a parvenu or interloper, though actually he came from a far better social background than theirs. Pompous, self-important bastards, he would show them! He laughed inwardly. Ever since school, he had enjoyed sowing trouble.

Next it was necessary to find the right lawyers to assist Fielding. He was a powerful and effective advocate, but he would expect the spadework to have been done for him. The choice fell between McKinnon, Filigree, Bratt, Gorbinge, on the one hand, and Colbert, Smithers, ffynch-Roberts on the other. Greenweather chose the latter because he had been at school with ffynch-Roberts, who had always been brilliant if a little wayward. He was another patron saint, or at least patron lawyer, of unpopular, radical or lost causes. Possessed of a solid fortune irrespective of what he earned (which was a lot), assisting those who wanted to undermine the social order on which his fortune was founded was his way of expiating his undeserved good luck. Not, of course, that he believed that the foundations ever would, or could, really be undermined. Besides, he had enough faith in himself to know that, whatever happened, he would come out on top.

None of this meant, of course, that he was not an excellent and diligent lawyer; his freedom from economic pressure permitted him a thoroughness that was at least as important as brilliance. He set to work on the case, requisitioning papers, reading evidence from many sources, mastering arguments. One of the pleasures of the case was that, if successful, it would expand the boundaries of the law and mark an historic turning point.

The case was ready, the prosecution was brought, the date of the trial set. It was represented everywhere as the battle of good and evil, of the public versus the private interest. In the dock were six men who were at the pinnacle of command of Big Tobacco. Their companies accounted for ninety per cent of national sales of the accursed, or at any rate reviled, leaf.

Ranged on the other side, for the defence, was Sir Stansby Renwick, Q.C., an advocate of long experience at the commercial bar. He was skilled at whitening the black and blackening the white, and famous for his ability to make a witness say exactly the opposite of what he had said moments before. This he achieved quite without aggression, indeed with a kind of buttery courtesy that narrowly missed being oily. A witness whose testimony he had just destroyed felt grateful to him for having done so, not realising that he had been made to look an unprincipled scoundrel. If Sir Stansby had cross-examined George Washington, the latter would have emerged from the stand with a reputation as a pathological liar.

But Greenweather had realised that legal action by itself would not be enough. What was needed in addition was some form of popular agitation and even a movement. Besides being a good thing in itself – raising consciousness and bringing CASH to the forefront of the public mind, in so far as the public had a mind – it would intimidate the jury into passing the correct verdict. And what actual arguments could those opposed to the aims of CASH put up? That it was economically advantageous that people should die early of diseases caused by smoking and therefore did not live to draw their pensions? Who would dare to argue such a thing after CASH's public relation firm, Thorsby, Crippen and Company, had managed to place assorted widows in the public eye, until they had become familiar faces to the whole population? A sob on television was worth more than an entire philosophical treatise.

Thorsby, Crippen had been the provocateurs of many alterations in public opinion, which they considered a purely technical problem. Unanimity was not their goal, but a change in atmosphere, so that even opponents of whatever view they were paid to promote began to shift their ground. They accepted your premises and were put on the defensive: and a man on the defensive always appears shifty to the public, as if he had something to hide, for example a hidden financial interest, however sincere or honest he might be. Your side – that is to say, the side that paid you – looked by comparison like knights in shining armour, fighting impossible odds but convinced because of its own rectitude of final victory in a world in which injustice, however long triumphant, must in the end yield to truth.

What was needed was activism, the kind that had made fur coats disappear from the streets and veal from the butchers' shops. Smokers must be shamed and the purveyors of tobacco exposed as merchants of death. Thorsby, Crippen was careful to maintain and cultivate its contacts in activist circles, journalists and the like, the kind of people for whom agitation was a way of life, a *raison d'être*. And since the world was what it had always been, deeply unsatisfactory, there was always something to agitate about.

That is how and why smokers began to receive insults in the street and purveyors of tobacco had posters pasted to their shopfronts and slogans spray-painted on their walls. Anyone seen smoking would be harangued by an activist for bringing chronic disease upon himself and thereby wasting public money on care that could be spent on more deserving cases. But the purveyors, being commercial and therefore the more culpable, were the favoured targets. Activists would enter premises in which tobacco was sold, ask for a packet of cigarettes, and then accuse the shop-owner or assistant of being an accessory to murder. If the assistant said that he was only doing his job, the activist would reply, 'Only obeying orders, are you?' Deaths from diseases caused by tobacco were likened to the Holocaust (except that they had killed far more people), and anyone who tried to argue back was called a holocaust-denier.

The offices of the tobacco companies were picketed day and night. However vigilant the police, however many cameras were installed, the spray-painters managed to paint 'Profit kills' and 'Dealers in murder' on the buildings. Employees had daily to run a gauntlet of demonstrators calling them murderers or prostitutes as they entered or left. Sometimes they were pelted with eggs – free-range, and given to children to throw, to avoid arrests for assault. They claimed dry-cleaning costs from the companies, which at first they refused until a newspaper exposed their meanness.

The companies moved their offices, and then removed all public signs of their name, as if ashamed of themselves; but the activists had moles or sympathisers in the companies, those who were disgruntled with them for some reason or other, and they soon informed the activists who re-formed outside the new premises. Moving offices, then, while expensive, resulted in nothing but the shortest respite and made the companies look ridiculous, like dinosaurs in an age of small, agile mammals. And though the companies were as profitable as ever, their share prices fell, as churches and universities divested themselves of any funds that held them. Financial commentators wrote of them as if they were the heroines of operas dying of tuberculosis, singing a swansong before expiry. Moreover, the source of the majority of their remaining profits, exports to the Third World, was grist to the activists' mill. They were accused of exporting death to the poor.

The agitation spread, for example to insurance or other companies that retained their shares in the tobacco companies. Their holdings were large for individuals but small for giant financial institutions, and it was worth their while to sell them in order to disembarrass themselves of the nuisance of demonstrators on their doorsteps. Of course, they did not admit that they had been intimidated: on the contrary, they claimed they had been motivated by purely ethical or commercial considerations, but no one was deceived.

At first, the activists were unopposed. Who, after all, was in favour of premature death, especially of the poor many more of whom smoked than the rich? If you defended Big Tobacco, you murdered the small man: for he who condones the means wills the end. Naturally, in the privacy of people's thoughts, or in drunken conversations in the pubs, things were different; there was dissent from what any decent person would say, or dare to say, in public. But everywhere else, Big Tobacco was guilty as charged.

The trial of the directors for murder changed the situation.

At first, the prosecution had it all its own way. Xavier Fielding, Q.C., was a virtuoso.

'Trials,' he said at sophisticated dinner parties where everyone, *ex officio*, admired him, 'are performances as much as plays. They have to be rehearsed and directed.'

Among his first witnesses after his opening address to the jury was Mrs Green. Of all the early widows who had come forward in response to an appeal, she was found to be one of the most fluent, spontaneous and credible sobbers. She didn't overdo it to the point of incoherence, however; that was important. Her sobs would not altogether drown out her words, like sauce destroying the flavour of fish. Sobs had to be appropriate rather than hysterical. Mrs Green was what Fielding called 'a natural'.

Her husband had died of cancer after eight years of marriage – eight years of blissful and unblemished happiness, of course, except for the last two and a half years of fatal illness – leaving two orphans. Mr Green had started to smoke at the age of twelve, and because nicotine had proved so addictive to him, he had been unable from the first to stop. He had made valiant and titanic efforts to do so, but had always failed. And then, when his cancer had been diagnosed, it was too late: there was no point then in stopping. The irreparable damage had been done.

Mrs Green, a small woman, was dressed if not quite in black

(Fielding thought that would be too obvious), at least in dark and sober clothes. In a low voice, without rhetorical flourish apart from her occasional sob, she described how, while her husband was still able to work, she had decided to be a housewife because she thought it better for the children to have their mother at home. In other circumstances, Fielding would have thought this contemptible, the product of the immemorial brainwashing of women, but here it served his purpose: tobacco had destroyed this domestic idyll. Fielding led her gently through her harrowing story, punctuated by brief pauses for sobs, but not too many, and only one requiring an adjournment of five minutes. Although Fielding had a reputation for tiger-like ferocity and terrier-like persistence, he was also capable of compassion when necessary and avuncular kindness. You would have thought he felt his witness's suffering as his own.

At the end of his examination-in-chief, it was Sir Stansby's turn.

'No questions,' he said, and sat down.

There was a stir in the courtroom: but Sir Stansby had decided that, however preposterous Widow Green's story, to question her aggressively or even disbelievingly would alienate the jury even if he attained some kind of intellectual victory over her. To win an argument was not the same as winning a case. To have pointed out that her late husband knew perfectly well when he started smoking that he ought not to have done so, that he was transgressing the rules – indeed, that transgression had been nine tenths of the pleasure of smoking, at least to begin with – and that he had been all his life aware of the harms and dangers of smoking; and furthermore that millions of people had given up smoking once they had started, suggesting weakness of will on his part; all this, interrupted by the inevitable sobs of the widow would have marked him out from the first as a hard-hearted and mercenary calculating machine, unlike his so-compassionate opponent, the brave warrior on behalf of the small people, the defenceless victims of commercial intrigue and greed. Tears were to logic what tsunamis were to palm-front huts, and initial impressions could last for the duration of a trial, never mind what came afterwards. Sir Stansby had long decided that he would rely more on his own witnesses for the defence than on the destruction of the prosecution's witnesses.

Fielding brought many kinds of expert to the witness box. There were epidemiologists to establish the statistical link between smoking and practically every known disease, and pathologists, toxicologists and biochemists to demonstrate that the link was not merely statistical but causal. They were men of the highest scientific calibre who spoke calmly, dispassionately and without the faintest hint of *parti pris*. Their assurance in their own expertise meant that they did not have to raise their voices to make themselves heard; the plainness of their delivery was the guarantee of their authority. Of course, their evidence was, in essence, common knowledge and quite uncontested, least of all by Sir Stansby. To have tackled them would have looked like nit-picking at best, and obscurantism at worst, as if he were defending the indefensible and was now desperate.

The next step in Fielding's argument was that Big Tobacco had not only known the fatal horrors of their products, but had long sought dishonestly to conceal them from public knowledge. This, too, could hardly be disputed: the evidence had long been known and publicised.

Again, Sir Stansby's cross-examination was neither very aggressive nor of long duration. He contented himself by asking how long the harms of tobacco had been known to the public. He asked Professor Hoolie, Fielding's expert on addiction, what he thought Mark Twain meant by his famous remark, that giving up smoking was the easiest thing in the world because he'd done it hundreds of times. The professor was forced to admit, though only after prevarication, that it implied smoking was addictive. 'But,' added the professor, 'not everyone knows of Mark Twain's witticism.'

'He was a popular author, was he not?' asked Sir Stansby.

'I don't know,' replied Professor Hoolie before Fielding could object. 'I am not a literary expert.'

'Let me put it another way,' said Sir Stansby. 'Mark Twain was not a famous researcher in the field of addiction, was he?'

'No.'

'Thank you,' said Sir Stansby, gathering his gown about him as he sat down, a gesture that he had scored a point, or thought that he had.

The case for the prosecution was now complete. It was in outline simple: tobacco killed and the people in charge of Big Tobacco had always known that it did, but continued for the sake of profit, both individual and collective, to sell it. It was irrelevant that smokers were complicit in their own deaths. You cannot consent to be murdered.

It was now the turn of the defence. Its first witness was a professor of economics who had estimated the revenue the government had gathered from tobacco over the years. It was a vast sum.

'And have you estimated how many times more is that sum than the profits of the principal tobacco companies?'

'Yes.'

'How many times?'

'Seven or eight.'

Sir Stansby paused to let it sink in.

'Let me be sure that I have understood you correctly,' he then said. 'The government has derived seven or eight times more revenue from the sales of tobacco products than have the tobacco companies?'

'That is so,' said the professor, looking down modestly.

There was a stir in the court. Sir Stansby was implying that if the directors of Big Tobacco were murderers, they were only the accomplices of members of the government, past, present and probably to come.

Fielding rose. He did not speak straight away, as if gathering his capacious thoughts. It did not do to appear too clever to a jury.

'I suppose, professor,' he said, 'that you accept the evidence of the experts as to the harms done by tobacco.'

'I have no reason or expertise to doubt them.'

'And many of the diseases caused by tobacco are chronic?'

'I believe so.'

'And treatment of those diseases may extend over many years?'

'Yes.'

'Requiring perhaps many hospital admissions?'

'Yes.'

'And such diseases may greatly curtail a person's working life?'

'Yes.'

'So that it would be fair to say that both in the medical costs and the costs of lost production, the habit of smoking has a large cost to the government?'

'To the taxpayer, yes.'

'And these costs exceed in total the tax revenue raised from tobacco?'

'There is no agreement on that. It is true that the majority of economists think that the costs exceed the revenue, but there are others who think the opposite.'

'How so?'

'People who smoke die several years before those who don't. They die nearer the end of their working lives and therefore cost less in pensions, to which they have contributed during their working lives.'

'So you are saying that the government and pension funds benefit from the premature death of its citizens caused by smoking?'

'Yes.'

'I see.' Fielding sat down, glancing theatrically at his opponent, after having intimated his disgust at such an argument. He held in reserve the argument, or truism, that two wrongs don't make a right: that killing is no less murder because someone else has taken part in it.

Sir Stansby rose to re-examine.

'No one has ever suggested that it is in the tobacco companies' interest that consumers of their products should die prematurely?'

'No.'

'On the contrary, it is in their interests that consumers

should live as long as possible, especially as fewer people than ever are taking up the habit?'

'Yes.'

'Thank you.'

Sir Stansby sat down, returning his opponent's glance. They belonged to the same club, but were not great friends.

By far the most important witness for the defence, upon whose performance the whole trial would turn, was Sir Patrick O'Flynn, chief executive officer of the British and Universal Tobacco Company, known to stockbrokers as BUTS. He was a pugnacious Irishman who had started in the company as a sweeper and office boy, but had risen by native cunning, determination, ruthlessness, and mastery of every kind of detail relative to the company's business to the very top of its tree. He was known as an uncompromising defender of the industry, wheeled out as it were to defend it whenever there was a public attack upon it.

He climbed into the witness-box like a prize fighter entering the ring. After a few formal questions establishing his identity and describing his distinguished career (emphasising his humble origins), and pointing out that he had been widely honoured for his services to exports, Sir Stansby came to the heart of the matter.

'You have, of course, as chief executive of one of the largest tobacco companies in the world, studied the scientific evidence that concerns smoking?'

'Yes.'

Sir Stansby established by his questions that the witness was innocent of having ordered scientists to breed tobacco plants with higher concentrations of nicotine the better and quicker to addict smokers to the habit. He had never authorised such a thing: it had all been done before he became chief executive. Moreover, his company – and as far as he was aware all other companies – had always scrupulously complied with all government regulations and demands. If those regulations and demands were deficient, that was not his fault. The blame lay elsewhere.

'At any time, anywhere in the world, have you or your company, knowingly or unknowingly, done anything illegal?'

'No.'

'At any time, anywhere in the world, have you or your company, knowingly or unknowingly, sought to kill anyone or procure his early death?'

'No.'

Everyone knew that Fielding's cross-examination would be crucial to the case. As the time for it approached, the anti-smoking agitation grew more fervent. In Rotherham, a corner shop owned by a Pakistani that sold cigarettes to the impoverished local population was attacked and set alight, leading to accusations of racism: so then the activists burned down a luxurious supermarket that also sold cigarettes, thus refuting the accusation. And a large crowd of demonstrators or mob, as one newspaper which had changed sides in the tobacco war now called it, having realised that sixty per cent of its readers, being uneducated, smoked, some of them wearing balaclavas and military fatigues, as if planning military or guerrilla action, gathered outside the court. They banged drums and chanted continually, 'We're not joking, let's ban smoking,' and 'Killing for money isn't funny.' University students called for a one-day strike, to be extended if necessary, against smoking, at least of tobacco: to raise consciousness, they said. The more militant of them broke into administrative offices to check that the universities held no shares in tobacco companies, either directly or indirectly; and they wrecked the interior of one neo-gothic building because it had been donated to the university by a local tobacco magnate more than a hundred years earlier. They also knocked down his statue on the grounds that he was a mass-murderer and ought not to be commemorated. They demanded that the university made a rule that it would be a disciplinary offence to utter his name in the precincts of the university, and the vice-chancellor agreed. There was a small riot in the special collections room of the library when it was discovered that the magnate's papers were held there. They were taken out into the courtyard and burned, while the students chanted 'No more games, up in flames.' Unfortunately, quite by accident, the papers of an eighteenth century poet were burnt as well as those of the magnate, but one of the student leaders, a student of history, interviewed on television about this (wearing a balaclava), said that the study of history demonstrated that there was no progress without collateral damage and that in any case no one was interested in the eighteenth century poet who was a notorious reactionary, the study of whom was an elitist irrelevance to distract people from current social injustices.

Fielding began his cross-examination gently enough, just to demonstrate that he had no personal animus towards the witness. Juries didn't like it when advocates showed hostility from the first: it caused them to sympathise with the witness. They preferred moral indignation to build up gradually; and in any case, the advantage is always with the advocate, for the greatest fool can always ask more than the wisest man can know.

'Sir Patrick,' began Fielding courteously, 'I think it fair to say that you have worked for British and Universal Tobacco for a very long time?'

O'Flynn agreed, but he was not deceived by Fielding's apparent respect and amiability. He knew his kind of smiling assassin: if courtesy came, could hostility be far behind?

'And you rose quickly through the ranks?'

'Yes.'

'By your ability which was recognised?'

'I think so.'

It would have been absurd to deny it; in any case, some other explanation would have been worse. Fielding read out the positions he had held, including postings abroad, in research and marketing and finance, and in every important capacity. He had been on the board for more than twenty-five years.

'That's right, isn't it?' said Fielding.

O'Flynn agreed.

'So again it would be fair to say that from an early stage in your career you must have been party to the activities to the company in all their aspects?'

'Not all its aspects, no.'

'Well, let's see. Thirty years ago you were in charge of the company's advertising?'

'Yes, that is correct.'

'Do you recall the advertising slogan for the company's new Velvet brand?'

'Yes.'

'What was it?'

'New Velvet: smoother, milder, more sophisticated.'

'There was something more, was there not?'

'Yes.'

'What was it?'

'The type the young prefer.'

'The type the young prefer,' repeated Fielding, looking pointedly at the jury. 'The young then who are now suffering from angina and chronic bronchitis.'

He let it sink in and then returned to O'Flynn.

'So it would also be true to say that both the advertising and the brand were aimed at the young as a market?'

'Well, of course we wanted others to smoke as well.'

'Of course. But still it was aimed principally at the young?'

O'Flynn knew that Fielding was in possession of the company's internal documents and he had therefore been advised by Sir Stansby to agree quickly to anything he knew to be true, however damaging: for a quick admission is always much less damaging than one slowly extracted from a reluctant witness like a fish being landed on the river bank after a long fight. Such an admission created an indelible impression of guilt.

'Yes,' said O'Flynn.

'Let us turn now,' said Fielding, 'to the claim that Velvet brand was smoother and milder. In what way was Velvet brand smoother and milder?'

'It was low in tar. It is the tar content of cigarettes that is harmful to the lungs, or rather the chemicals that tar contains.'

'I am glad that you mentioned cancer. Is it not true that your company tried for years to deny that smoking caused lung cancer?'

'It never denied the statistical association. But statistical association is not causation, and such association was all, at first, that had been demonstrated.'

'But the connection between smoking and cancer was not only statistical, it was biologically plausible, was it not?'

'Plausible, yes, but plausibility is not proof. It is plausible that the sun goes round the earth, but it isn't true that the sun goes round the earth.'

'Nevertheless, biological plausibility added to strong statistical association is generally accepted as a criterion of a causative relationship, is it not?'

'It wasn't then. In fact, it was only accepted after and not before the connection had been proved experimentally, after which the company – and all other companies – did not deny it.'

'But the admission – or absence of denial, as you prefer to put it – was at the last possible moment, when it was no longer possible to do otherwise?'

'It was as soon as the causative link was proved, and neither before nor afterwards.'

'A very laudable sense of scientific rigour, I am sure,' said Fielding, again looking at the jury. They were a rabble, mostly, juries, and this one was no exception. Long gone were the days when juries dressed smartly to perform their greatest duty as citizens. They were drawn mainly from people who couldn't think of a good reason to be excused. They dressed as if they had just crawled out bed after a hard night before: but Fielding knew from experience that there was usually at least one among them who was alert and intelligent and who would guide the others. It was to him or her that he addressed his sarcasm. If one man smiled at it, Fielding was satisfied; and one man did smile at it.

'The tar content of Velvet brand, you say, was low?'

'Yes.'

'By comparison with what?'

Fielding was now springing like a tiger.

'With other brands.'

'In the same market, namely for the young?'

'Yes.'

'How much lower?'

'Ten per cent on average.'

'Ten per cent. Was that enough to make an appreciable difference to the rate of cancer?'

'I am not sure.'

'You're not sure. Take a look at this graph, will you?'

Fielding handed him a graph that plotted the rate of cancer against the tar content of cigarettes.

'The difference made by your ten per cent is barely perceptible, isn't it?'

'That depends on the scale of the graph,' said O'Flynn. 'You can make large differences look small and small differences look large by choosing your scale and how to present the graph.'

Fielding handed the graph to the jury.

'Are you seriously suggesting,' he asked O'Flynn as he did so, 'that the difference in the rate of cancer in this case was large?'

'Every life is important to the person whose life is spared.'

Fielding sprang again.

'Precisely,' he said. 'That is why these charges against you are serious. Hecatombs of people have fallen victim to your products and, as you rightly say, each one who died was important to himself – and to everyone around him.'

Fielding paused for effect, and then said:

'Let us now turn not to the tar but the nicotine content of your Velvet brand.' He had some papers before him, and pretended to look at them, though he knew their content perfectly. 'It was very high, wasn't it?'

'There were other brands that were higher.'

'How many brands were higher?'

O'Flynn looked down, as if he had suddenly discovered something of interest below him.

'One,' he said.

'One,' repeated Fielding, with stage disgust. 'And that brand was called Smooth, was it not?'

'Yes.'

'And who manufactured Smooth brand?'

'We did.'

'So your company, the company of which you are chief executive, manufactured and marketed the two brands with the highest nicotine content, one of them aimed specifically at the young. And I think I am right in saying – correct me if I'm wrong – that Velvet and Smooth brand were launched at the same time?'

'Almost.'

'And you were already chief executive at the time?'

'Yes.'

Fielding appeared to gather his thoughts.

'How did it come about that the two brands had higher nicotine contents than others?'

'Tobacco leaves with higher nicotine content were used.'

'And that was not by chance, was it?'

'No.'

'How did it happen?'

'Leaves were selected.'

'They were not just selected, were they?'

'Nicotine content varies naturally between strains.'

'But it wasn't just natural variation, was it? Your company actually bred plants with high nicotine content, didn't it?'

'Yes.'

'When you were at the helm?'

'Yes.'

'Thank you, Sir Patrick.' Fielding shuffled his papers. 'Now, if I may, I should like to ask you what is the substance that makes smoking addictive?'

'Nicotine. But addiction is not destiny. Millions of people have stopped smoking...'

'Thank you, Sir Patrick,' interrupted Fielding brusquely. 'Just answer the questions I put to you.'

O'Flynn, used to command, and known for his swift temper and imperiousness, looked venomously at Fielding. He never forgot an injury or insult; he had been a street fighter, as it were, a man who had clawed his way up, not like Fielding who had been born with a silver spoon in his mouth, who now thought of himself so superior morally, intellectually and socially!

'What was the purpose of breeding and selecting leaves of higher nicotine content?' Fielding resumed.

'To please customers. Smokers prefer them.'

'Smokers prefer them? But it was not just a question of preference, was it, Sir Patrick?'

'What do you mean?'

'I mean the higher the nicotine content, the faster and more strongly the smokers become addicted. Is that not so?'

'I know of no evidence to that effect.'

'We have ordered documents from your company to prove it, and prove that you knew it.'

'Is that a question?'

'I can make it a question if you like.'

O'Flynn was silent.

'Then I can take it as read?'

'Yes.'

'So it amounts to this, does it not? That you targeted young people to get them to take up the habit, and plied them with a brand that would addict them especially quickly?'

'Quicker,' said O'Flynn, emphasising the last syllable. 'No one is addicted to cigarettes quickly. It takes time, determination and practice. Moreover, surveys show that teenagers know before they start that smoking is addictive.'

'Would you advise your own children to take it up?'

'I wouldn't advise them to take up many other things.'

'Your advertisements, then, were for other people's children?'

'They informed them of what was available. They did not advise them to take up smoking. They only suggested which brand to smoke if they smoked at all.'

'But your object was to increase the sales of your company to them?'

'Of course. To switch to our brands.'

'And the object of your brands was to addict them as quickly as possible?'

'That is your interpretation.'

'The jury will draw its own conclusions.' Fielding paused

again. 'I want now to move on to something else. It is true, is it not, that the proportion of young people in this country who take up smoking has been falling for many years?'

'Yes, but it has flattened out recently.'

'Yes, all right, but at a much lower level than formerly?'

'Yes.'

'But yet the sales of your company have continued to rise?'

'Yes.'

'How is that?'

'Exports.'

'Exports,' repeated Fielding. 'Mainly to the Third World, to poor countries?'

'As they become richer, they are our fastest-growing market.'

'In other words, you are preserving if not increasing your profits at the expense of impoverished people whom you encourage to take up a fatal habit?'

'The poor of the world are not nearly as poor as they were. In fact...'

But Sir Patrick got no further. Someone from the public gallery – for justice had to be seen to be done – rushed forward, reached the witness box, drew a large knife that had somehow been smuggled in despite security precautions (later investigations would suggest an accomplice in the court canteen) and struck O'Flynn several times in the chest and abdomen, shouting, 'Death to death dealers! People before profit!'

At first, it was as if everyone in the court had been administered a paralysing agent: short-acting, though, for its effect wore off quickly and turned into a kind of convulsant. Chaos reigned. Some rushed to assist O'Flynn, without really knowing how to do so, and got in the way of each other; the only doctor among them a small man in his mid-fifties, could not get through the press of people. Others concentrated on apprehending the killer – it was soon obvious that Sir Patrick was dead – and in this they were more successful than the first-aiders. They prevented him from escaping, as he had clearly intended to do, more by sheer numbers than skill: they simply blocked his way. The judge, meanwhile, had been ushered from the bench to safety.

He was later accused of cowardice, but what he was supposed to have done in the circumstances was not specified.

An ambulance was called and the police arrived with machine-guns, but unfortunately there was no one to shoot. The killer was taken into custody and the main immediate task was to clear the courtroom of the spectators, as they had become. There were at least eighty eye-witnesses to the events, which made it harder, not easier, for the police.

The news of the stabbing to death of Sir Patrick O'Flynn soon reached the demonstrators outside the court. They began to cheer, and if they had been Arabs or Africans, they would have ululated. One among them thought of a chant: 'One down, the rest to go! One down, the rest to go!' They jumped up and down and punched the air. They were filmed on television and some of them waved or held up the V for Victory sign for the viewers. One of them was interviewed. He said that the Movement was peaceful and did not agree with murder; but O'Flynn had been responsible for the deaths of millions. The struggle to make the world smoke-free would continue.

The murder was grist to the media's mill. There were heated discussions on the ethics of smoking. Orden Jebb, the media's favourite young radical, who had early in adolescence adopted a proletarian appearance and intonation in protest against his family's bourgeois pretensions which went back several generations, appeared everywhere. Though he was still young, he looked much younger and exuded youthful moral certainty like a secretion; he smiled only with difficulty. As long as there was a single injustice left in the world to fight – and nowadays you couldn't hide behind the excuse that you didn't know about it – he thought it very wrong to be contented. Contentment was complacency, and complacency was complicity.

His main point, which he reiterated constantly (despite his youth, he was a great reiterator) was that it was quite wrong to emphasise a single death like that of O'Flynn when every day thousands were suffering or even dying as a result of O'Flynn's activities – not, of course, that the system would fail to replace him. It was typical of capitalist morality to concentrate attention on a single dramatic event and to disregard entirely the underlying structure. O'Flynn had been merely an individual, a symptom rather than the disease. Jebb wished, despite his multiple appearances on every medium of communication, that people would stop talking about what he called the assassination, and start talking about the politics of tobacco and other harmful commodities such as farmed salmon. He said that, from now on, he would personally join the demonstrators until smoking was outlawed and the directors of tobacco companies were in prison.

The agitation did not die down after O'Flynn's death. There were meetings calling for the release of the killer, an anarcho-vegetarian called, or calling himself, Old Boddo. He had served a prison sentence before, for having with a group of friends broken into the zoo at night and released the crocodiles from captivity.

Then came another killing. Activists broke into the home of the retired chief executive of Continental (formerly Colonial) Tobacco, British and Universal's greatest competitor, in the Cotswold village of Markworth St Gildas and battered him to death, which wasn't difficult because he was in his mid-eighties. The interlopers painted slogans on the honey-coloured stone walls of his beautiful house: JUSTICE FOR SMOKERS! and PROFITS UP IN SMOKE!

It was after this second assassination, as Jebb called it, pointing out that even two deaths did not weigh in the balance against all the harms of tobacco, that the English Liberties Defence League began to attack the anti-smoking demonstrators. The activists of the league were armed with baseball bats; they were shaven-headed, aged between eighteen and forty, whose only previous exercise, despite their football kit, was in pub brawls. Their first attack, out of the blue, was on the demonstrators outside British and Universal Tobacco's new headquarters, which at the time was being addressed by a Member of Parliament who was demanding that the tobacco companies compensate all the widows and widowers they had created. He had introduced a bill to this effect, but of course it had not been debated: as Jebb repeatedly pointed out, the system would never allow it.

Two large white vans drew up and about forty men clambered out wearing balaclavas like many of the demonstrators. Some wore white T-shirts with the cross of St George. They set about the demonstrators with their baseball bats, and though heavily outnumbered, the effect of surprise more than compensated for this. By the time they jumped back into their vans and made their getaway, about fifty of the demonstrators were sprawled on the ground, some with fractured skulls or other injuries. It was a great victory.

Jebb was everywhere again (everywhere that is, in a technical sense), alleging that the police had been aware of the impending attack and done nothing to prevent it or intervene in it. He said they were in league with the League, and called for massive protests for the right to protest, and for the right to be protected while doing so. It was the most basic right of all, he said.

Then the English Liberties Defence League, composed of men far uglier than Nature had made them, tried to demonstrate. Jebb called on the authorities to ban the demonstration because it represented a provocative threat to public order, being fascist in nature, Fascists were trying, by definition, to destroy the people's freedom, and therefore there should be no freedom for them. Xavier Fielding, who was not averse to publicity, agreed.

But the day following one of his appearances on television, he was attacked and left for dead outside his chambers. It had never occurred to him that he might be in danger: his existence had always been too secure for that. He was not killed but so severely brain-damaged that he would never again be free of life-support, let alone appear in a court case. The hospital advised that the machines on which he now depended be turned off and he be left to die with dignity; but his long-term consort, something of a film starlet (he had been married and divorced three times) started a campaign to prevent the hospital from doing this because she said there was a chance he might recover and he was a man of national importance. As a result of this campaign, Fielding was removed from the list of patrons of the Right to Death Society (known as RIDS).

The students mobilised and went on strike. They discovered to their chagrin that no one noticed, or noticed only to draw mocking attention to the fact than no one noticed. But the radicals among them were not discouraged; on the contrary, they saw it as evidence of the need to raise consciousness, as they called their own ideas. And the most radical of the radicals among them decided on the propaganda of the deed.

The first target was a very old, wood-panelled cigar-shop in the heart of clubland. About ten of them descended on it with crow-bars (baseball bats were the weapon of the enemy) and destroyed it beyond repair. The business, a century and a quarter old, and already in decline, closed for good. Then Cadence Pennyfeather, an ardent defender of the rights of animals, with long experience of 'direct action' against laboratories, drew public attention to the futility of action against supply while demand remained high. She suggested that the tactic used so successfully against wearers of fur coats – spraying them with paint, for example – be applied to smokers. As a result, groups of vigilantes went forth in towns and cities, looking for smokers in the street or outside buildings (where they had long been forced to gather), and sprayed paint on them. After all, they were complicit with Big Tobacco, which was dependent on them and their ilk. If it were not for them, there would be no profits for Big Tobacco to make, who then would not have had the means to sell their wares to the innocent and vulnerable in the Third World.

The English Liberties Defence League, however, did not accept this passively. Its membership grew, and little groups of them took to beating up students wherever they found them. The niceties of students' individual responsibility were lost on them; for them, all students were the same. They were privileged arrogant knowalls who had to be taught a lesson. It served them right, whatever they'd done or not done. It was a pleasure to educate them with baseball bats.

Oren Jebb did not remain silent or inactive, of course. Now was not the moment for neutrality, which was a form of fascism, he said. Everyone had to choose sides, for liberation or enslavement. It was time for a showdown in a society divided by injustice and inequality, to destroy the forces of division once and for all. This included the police, who were clearly biased in favour of the fascists, despite their claims to fairness and even-handedness because both sides were getting away with murder. The police, said Jebb, knew who the fascists were: why had they not arrested them? The answer was obvious.

The government vacillated, and then decided to act. It passed a law making it illegal to be critical of students or derogatory of them as a whole. The first man to be prosecuted under the new law was an old man in a pub, one of the regulars who was overheard by two students to say 'Students! F... ing spoilt brats, if you ask me!' The students, who later testified that they had felt very threatened by this, called the police on their phones. The police arrived in force almost at once, dressed in riot gear, and with two vehicles suitable for carrying violent people away. Three policemen and a policewoman, dressed in stab-proof vests that gave them the appearance of living corpses in a horror film, and with belts festooned with gas-canisters, manacles and truncheons, muscled their way through the drinkers and grabbed a man who fitted the description supplied by the students over the phone, until someone told them he was the wrong man. They demanded to know who the right man was, and when he was pointed out to them they rushed at him as if he were trying to escape. Meanwhile, another policeman found the students and took a statement from them.

The police objected to bail because the old man was an alcoholic and they thought he might not answer to bail. He was remanded to prison, therefore, and later sentenced to four years' imprisonment. The judge said he was making an example of him, for this was no time to make defamatory remarks against students, even if uttered facetiously while drunk.

A few small demonstrations in his favour were held, but quickly dispersed by students chanting 'There is no date for speech of hate!' and 'No freedom for fascists!'

A member of the English Liberties Defence League drove

past a college in a northern town just as the students were emerging from the day's lectures and sprayed them with bullets from an automatic weapon. Twelve were killed and seventeen injured. There was singing and cheering that night in the Lamb and Flag, in which members of the League (as well as the unemployed) were known to gather: that is, until a bomb went off, killing nineteen people and injuring an unspecified number of others, suppressed by the government to avoid panic.

Soon there were such outrages almost every day. Students barricaded themselves inside colleges and universities, where they played at military training. They were attacked in the street whenever they were outnumbered. The government imposed censorship on news and commentary that only fed rumour: and everyone knew he was in danger, if only as a bystander or witness to an incident. Power transmission stations began to be blown up, though by whom was not clear. Speculation on this was rife: it depended upon who and what type of people were most affected by the resultant power cuts. The police did not venture from their stations for fear of attack, and when they were fire-bombed by arsonists, the fire brigade was attacked en route for its revolutionary or counter-revolutionary bias. Barricades and blocks appeared in the streets, and goods were requisitioned from shops that were said to be profiteering from shortages. Money began to lose its value and barter became the order of the day.

The government declared a state of emergency, but that changed nothing. Then it called in the army to enforce the curfew. At first, those who broke it were merely arrested, and sometimes beaten; but this was not sufficient to deter curfew-breakers, so they were now to be shot on sight. The first person to be killed under this new dispensation was a demented old lady in a nightdress who habitually wandered out at dusk. There was a demonstration in the town where she was shot, but this was dispersed by a short fusillade by the army.

Field-Marshal Jennifer (formerly John) Haxton-Perry mounted a coup and announced over the television and radio that from now on she was in charge. She was now known (secretly) as Miss Whiplash in the army – she had left it until late in her career to change sex, when she was already a Major-General. The upper echelons had been anxious to demonstrate that it was not hide-bound by prejudice as its critics alleged, and therefore quickly promoted her. However, by no means everyone in the army, particularly the lower ranks, was happy with the course of events or accepting of the change. In fact, acceptance did not run very deep, and after the coup, the army divided into two factions: the Loyalists and the Traditionalists, which began to fight one another. The Loyalists obeyed Field-Marshal Jennifer, the Traditionalists obeyed General Podmore, who had hated Haxton-Parry even before her sex-change. Loyalty was no longer traditional, and Tradition was no longer loyal.

Meanwhile, Oren Jebb had gone into noisy, conspicuous and much-publicised hiding: in a revolutionary situation, it would have been a disgrace and humiliation not to have done so, or to have felt that he did not need to do so. To be a target was a vindication of all that he had ever done or said. In other circumstances, he might have been somewhat sympathetic to Field Marshal Jennifer, indeed he had written a column welcoming her sex-change; but she had betrayed the movement by her authoritarianism, her military mindset trumping her gender dysphoria.

Silence descended on the population, for anything you said could be recorded and published on telephones. It was safest to say nothing, for there was now a violent group opposed to any opinion that could be expressed: both vegetarians and anti-vegetarians had their militias, pro- and anti-student groups, drinkers and teetotallers. Everything was regarded as sinister or bad by one group or other; everything anyone said was believed 'really' to mean something else, unless it was held to mean what it said. No one knew who his enemies were or might be; there were smiling assassins everywhere. Vigilance without being quite sure what you were looking for became the essence of survival. You might be struck down anywhere, even if you were not a target, as you entered a station, as you crossed the road, as you walked past a parked car, as you entered your place of work.

Now there was a war of each against all. Who was attacking whom, and what for? No one fully understood. But at least no one smoked any more, and deaths from bronchitis declined. The only smoke was from buildings.

EASEFUL DEATH

IS COMPANY having become by far the largest producer and distributor in the country of cannabis, ecstasy and khat, the people's billionaire (as Robert Barons liked to call himself) decided to start a chain of thanatoria, luxury spas to which those who were tired of life could go and be relieved of their lives in the gentlest and most comfortable way. There was a demand for it, he thought; if not, it could be created.

The public would have to be prepared and the government lobbied: but it had been the same, indeed a long hard struggle, with cannabis, ecstasy and khat. Barons decided to retain the services of Professor R. S. Failson, the media philosopher, who was able to convince anyone of anything, and its opposite also. His long, flowing, silky white hair would have been an argument in itself, even if he had not been the most fluent man in England.

Barons and Failson met in an expensive restaurant with a private room. Barons outlined his ideas to the professor, including the offer of five per cent of the shares in the thanatoria if his public promotion of the cause were successful (Baron's had thought about ten percent, but decided that five per cent would be sufficient).

The two men were very different, but both had cultivated their instant recognisability. Barons, though he was now in his sixties, dressed as if he were still nineteen; his curly locks were still as auburn as they had been then; only the deep creases in his smooth skin perpetually tanned by the sun of his Indian Ocean tax hideaway, let him down. His smile, full of teeth like bleached tombstones, seemed to fill his entire face except for his eyes. His manner was unfailingly familiar and ingratiating, whether he was trying to recruit someone or drive him into bankruptcy. He pawed his interlocutors like a dog who had known only indulgence from the human race.

Despite his Leonardo da Vinci-type hair, Failson wore suits with a collar and tie in all his public appearances (which were many): in that way, he could appeal to two audiences at once, or thought he could. Originally as specialist in Duns Scotus, he moved into popularity and celebrity with his best-selling books such as *Can Worms Suffer?* and *Do Fish Think?* Books then flowed from his pen like water through a leaking roof. But he was best-known for his view that parents should not be allowed to bring up a child in any religion or even broach the subject until they, the children, were fourteen (the new voting age, for which he had also campaigned). Just because he could answer both sides of any question with equal facility did not mean that he believed in nothing. He wanted to liberate Mankind from irrationality.

The dinner went well. Fortunately, they were Napoleons of different empires, and any acrimony between them could wait until later. In the meantime, they would mount a media campaign in favour of easeful death, which they were both well-placed to do. And Failson agreed to write a book, to be called *Last Rights,* about Man's inalienable right to die when, where and how he wished.

It took him three weeks and stirred, as it was intended to do, an intense controversy. Its argument was simple, and in two stages. First, he said, humans had the right, irrespective of their reasons and whether or not they availed themselves of it, to choose the hour and manner of their death. Those were morally obtuse who argued that since they had not asked to be born, nor could there be any right to be born, one was not the owner of one's life and could not therefore choose to end it, that one had a duty to continue it to its so-called natural end like a soldier who could not desert his lookout post. Indeed, the very arbitrariness of having been born, without consultation as to whether one wished to be, as a result of other people's decision or at least activity, added to rather than subtracted from the right to die as one chose. And it was obvious to anyone with the slightest acquaintance with the medical facts that some suffering of the terminally ill was perfectly pointless, useless and easily avoidable. The insistence that people should live out their so-called 'natural' span was philosophically incoherent because, where humans were concerned, either everything was natural, or nothing was. The demand that everyone should hang on to the bitter end, then, was merely sadistic. People had a right to have their suffering ended wherever it was possible, as it always was. Indeed, they had a moral duty to have their suffering ended, in so far as witnessing it caused suffering to others: to friends, relatives, medical and nursing staff. To continue to suffer when death was inevitable was mere egotism.

Once it was granted that the terminally-ill had a right and even a duty to ask for death, Failson moved on to the second stage of his argument: that it was clear that the right to die had to be extended to everyone else, for not to do so would be arbitrarily discriminatory. Why should only the dying have the best deaths? And what, in any case, was a terminal illness, how defined? An illness that would end in death in six months' time? Why not five, or seven? In any case, as any doctor could tell you, prognosis is not an exact science, and unlikely ever to become one. Some people with a poor prognosis survived much longer than expected, and others died unexpectedly. The only proper criterion for the right to die – that is to say, the right to be killed humanely and painlessly – was unbearable suffering.

But as any intelligent person would know (and all Failson's readers were intelligent), illness, terminal or otherwise, was not the only cause of unbearable suffering. Had not scientific studies amply demonstrated (yes, they had) that levels of suffering were poorly correlated with the extent or severity of physical pathology? There were myriad causes of human suffering: and who was the proper judge of whether or not the suffering was unbearable if not the sufferer himself? Suffering was ineradicably subjective, and therefore no one had the right to tell someone that his suffering was bearable. The only indisputably bearable suffering was the suffering of others: some people – psychopaths – could bear any amount of it.

In any case, said Failson, if we took the right to die seriously, people would not have to give any reason at all for wanting to die before being granted their wish. Their wish alone would be sufficient. Respect for their individual autonomy as human beings required that we did not question them about their reasons. As the great philosopher, David Hume, had said more than a quarter of a millennium ago, nobody would throw away his life for no good reason: though, added Failson, if he did so, it was nobody's business but his own.

Last Rights was reviewed everywhere. It was praised as both sophisticated and accessible, in Failson's best style. Failson was energetic for a man of his age, indeed for a man of any age. On television, on platforms, in newspapers and magazines, on the internet and social media, he brushed aside any arguments contrary to his own like noisome little insects. He was brilliant. Confronted one day by a doctor in an audience who said that if death on demand were a right, someone had a duty to provide it and he for one was not prepared on ethical grounds to do so, Failson did not retreat as others might have done but went on to the attack. The doctor, he said, speaking generically, was the agent of his patient; it was his duty always to ease his suffering. If a patient said that death was his only hope, who was the doctor to contradict him? Not to comply with his wishes was a breach of medical ethics, and any doctor not prepared to kill his patients on request should either leave the profession or go into a non-clinical branch. So combative and uncompromising was Failson, so scornful of his critics, that soon no one could be found willing to oppose him in public.

In the meantime, Barons founded and funded a charity (of which he remained studiously in the background) called the *Decent Death Association*. It employed the best advertising agency to make its advertisements, which soon appeared in every possible medium. It made short films of beautiful and affecting deaths (acted, of course, but faithful to the originals), and contrasted them with the horrors of 'natural' death among every possible kind of secretion and excretion, screams and groans. They made death seem like a positive pleasure rather than a mere relief, like a good night's sleep, only longer.

In his argument to prominent politicians, to whom he had almost instant access on his fleeting visits home (fleeting to avoid tax), Barons pointed out the obvious social and economic benefits of access to death on demand, and its reduction of many harms caused by the outmoded taboo against it. Every year, for example, there were untold thousands of botched suicide attempts, costing the health service many millions to treat. Here was a golden opportunity to reduce suffering while saving money. He suggested that to attempt suicide should become a crime again, subject to a heavy fine, once licensed thanatoria (he was open-minded, though, on what they should be called) were available everywhere. What good reason could anyone give for making a suicidal gesture when the real thing was on offer? When people tried to hang themselves and made a hash of it, they often ended up brain-damaged, imposing financial and emotional burdens on everyone around them. Thanatoria would separate the truly suicidal sheep from the merely histrionic goats.

As an old hand at political persuasion in favour of his schemes, Barons adapted what he said to his audience of the moment. To some he emphasised the economic savings, to others the extension of human rights, to yet others the reduction of human suffering or the reduction of the waste of environmentally-limited resources. But to whomever he spoke, it was with his habitual geniality, with his gash-like smile and dental display. To the leaders of parties and factions, he promised generous donations.

Of course, he also explained the need for proper regulation and control. No one would want fly-by-night thanatoria that would flout regulations or cut corners for lack of capital. Standards of everything would have to be high, from information systems to furnishing, from properly-trained staff to memorial gardens (Barons suggested that every thanatorium should have a minimum acreage, for aesthetic and security reasons, as well as of good taste, though he acknowledged that this would drive up the cost of establishing them). To those who were worried that the cost of death in thanatoria would be so high that only the rich could afford it, so that even in death there would be social injustice, he replied that death in thanatoria should be means-tested, with government subsidies for those unable to pay for themselves. Besides, the costs could be recovered from the estates of the deceased, which would rarely be so small that they did not cover the costs.

Between them, then, Frailson and Barons persuaded both public and politicians, and a bill was passed permitting the establishment of licensed thanatoria, one for every ten thousand deaths in the population per year, the minimum believed to be economically viable – struggling viability being an open invitation to abuse. Barons, of course, was ready with his plans, as no one else was: he knew that the first entrant into a field gained a natural and, if properly tended, unassailable advantage. A clever man who disguised his cunning by affability – for there was no quality more despised and hated in his country than cleverness – Barons had read the history of lunatic asylums built in the nineteenth century in rural areas just outside towns and cities. Barons decided that his thanatoria should be the asylum *de nos jours*: and even before the bill had been passed (as he knew it would) he bought up tracts of land suitable for them. He had his designs ready, too: he favoured a kind of neo-classical Californian Mediterranean style surrounded by cypresses, all quite formal but not off-puttingly so and quite friendly, with no pomposity but at the same time with a certain dignity. Death, after all, was a bit special, and the customers, or clients, as well as their relatives, would have to be made to feel important.

Barons decided on the same design for all his thanatoria and their furnishings. This had several advantages. First, it would save on architects' plans. Second, it would allow bulk purchase of fittings and furnishings, reducing unit costs. Third, and most important, it would establish a recognisable brand. Everyone would soon get to know what a Barons thanatorium looked like. Indeed, when people thought of thanatoria, they would immediately think of his. There would be no competition.

Thanks to his foresight – Barons had always been praised as a visionary, able to spot a trend as a surfer spots a wave – there was little delay between the passage of the law and the opening of the thanatoria. Failson was appointed as Director of Ethics, and medical directors found for each of the branches. They were mostly anaesthetists disgruntled by the pressure of work in the public service who were looking for an easier billet. What, after all, was death but an anaesthetic from which patients did not wake up, a great reduction in responsibility? Technicians could easily be trained up to the task of giving the fatal injections, the director being called in only when the physiologically recalcitrant refused to die with the calculated dose (it would be important financially to avoid overkill). Most of the work would be behind a desk, where so many doctors, after years of practice, wanted to be. Medical directorships of the thanatoria were suitable also for mothers who wanted a job-share for family and domestic reasons. In fact, Barons was much in favour of this arrangement because, except in his personal life, he had always been much in favour of sex equality. Besides, female medical directors would be good for the image of the thanatoria. They would seem more caring with women in charge, and make Barons more of a philanthropist than ever.

The first few deaths in the thanatoria were highly-publicised, as the launch of giant ocean-going liners used to be. There were heart-warming interviews with those whose long Calvary was soon to be so comfortably ended: some sobbed with gratitude. Relatives of the recently-killed related how beautiful, calm and peaceful it had all been. Those of the customers who were still able to eat had a last meal of their choice with a complimentary glass of champagne, including for up to three relatives in attendance. Everyone was full of praise for the arrangements, including those that preceded the deaths. Frailson had insisted that, on ethical grounds, legal advice be available to all postulants and their families. Indeed, having made a valid will was a precondition of acceptance for treatment. This, said Failson, would obviate any allegations that people were dying before they were really ready to do so. There were to be no stories of posthumous disputes because patients had died intestate; and for those who had made no will before seeking treatment, there was nothing like making a will for testing the consistency and sincerity of their desire for death.

As first there was but a single product, as Barons called it, offered by his thanatoria, for equality of the right to death had been one of the main arguments in favour of their establishment: it would not have done straight away to offer some deaths more luxurious than others. But business, while brisk enough, could not be expected to grow on the model of a single product; Barons had never been one to rest on his laurels, or allow his businesses to do so. He therefore asked the Director of Ethics, Frailson, to produce arguments for different deaths for different people, all of them remaining easeful of course, but varying in the trimmings and hence price. He would not bring these arguments to the fore but keep them in reserve for when the public learned that postulants for death could hire rooms, or suites of rooms, for a luxurious holiday before the final act, according to their taste and means. Failson, one of whose pedagogical methods had always been to get his students to argue for the opposite of what they said they really believed, duly obliged, and found fundamental arguments in favour of freedom of choice as the foundation of personal autonomy, the injustice of equality and so forth. With Failson's arguments at the ready, no one could ambush Barons successfully.

In addition to expansion and profits, however, Barons desired the limelight, so long as it did not penetrate too deeply into his affairs. Without limelight, he felt as if he had been buried alive. He had been so long in it that its absence suffocated him. He needed to be, directly or indirectly, in the news. Manipulation for him was as good as publicity.

He therefore engaged Sir Denny Spirt, recently retired First Secretary at the Treasury, to lobby his former colleagues to propose to the government a scheme of subsidised deaths. Using the best actuarial models possible, he proposed that those who were destined to be a charge on the public purse be offered lump-sum incentives to volunteer for death in the thanatoria, all expenses paid. The lump-sum, attractive to people who had never had a penny to their name, would be paid to the relatives of their choice after their deaths, a *quid pro quo* for the savings on their estimated pension and medical costs if they lived their 'natural' span. A quarter of the lump sum could be spent before the appointed hour to die, for example on a splendid coffin or a splendid farewell party. The contract to die was binding, but if the contracting party reneged on his undertaking, he would lose all his pension rights, as would the relatives designated to receive the bulk of the lump-sum; Failson objected to enforced deaths on the grounds that the public, given as ever to sentimentality, would not accept it. The lump-sum was set at just under half of the projected savings to the public purse, which had of course to be carefully calculated on a sliding scale.

While the proposal was debated, and before it was accepted, the thanatoria, but not Barons himself, were in the public eye. For the moment he thought that private lobbying was more effective than direct public exposure, in case it was thought that he had a pecuniary interest in the outcome of the deliberations. For the direct exposure he also desired, he would have to think of something else. This was no problem for his fertile brain.

He decided on a death channel and application for cable television and social media. Death, he argued (with Failson as tutor) was a normal part of life and for too long we had kept it hidden from view. This was, he said smilingly, *unhealthy*. It turned death into a taboo and therefore something to be feared. In the Middle Ages everyone had studied how to die well because they were so familiar with death. Not every idea from the past was bad, he said (having always extolled the future), and this was a good one, worthy of emulation and imitation in modern form. Familiarity in this case would not breed contempt but reason. To watch people die peacefully, even joyfully, would be an education. He would even advocate it as part of the school curriculum.

Of course, Barons believed none of this, if he could be said to believe anything at all, but it was good for public consumption. In any such enterprise it was advisable to win over the intelligentsia first with rationalisations. But what Barons really had in mind was game shows with prizes, competitions for death of the week, and so forth, all with himself as presenter and with the viewers voting for the winners. There was nothing like audience participation: it would be huge, and advertising revenue incalculable. The idea or the programmes themselves could be sold worldwide; Barons was never one to restrict his ambitions to a single country.

Death of the Week became one of the most popular programmes ever. It was sold in seventy-nine countries and watched illicitly in most of the others. Postulants for death related their life stories and sufferings, giving their reasons for wanting to die, and every week a million, a quarter million and a hundred thousand were awarded for the first, second and third places in the completion of most tragic story, as voted by the viewers. A subsidiary programme showed what the relatives of the winners did with the money they had won and the disputes it created. The money, it was found, usually melted away like snow in the sun. There had even been a family murder in a dispute over a quarter million. It was gripping.

Then came *Death of the Month* and *Death of the Year*, with even bigger prizes. *Death of the Year* was held on Christmas Day, when all the family gathered to watch.

It was Barons himself who presented the programmes and interviewed the postulants for death. He was a natural showman and he was by turns hilarious, genial and compassionate. He wanted to give people what they wanted. There was a minor scandal when it was revealed that some of the episodes were not what they seemed: because of his need to stay out of the country for tax reasons, some of the programmes were recorded months in advance and the deaths shown on them were not live, so to speak. But Failson did a magnificent job of heading off and silencing criticism. What was important, he said, was not the monthly periodicity of the shows, but the fact that they existed at all. It was their very existence that was educative, and in fact the prizes had been awarded on condition that the recipients did not reveal when they were paid. In any case, in the long run, the results were the same: no one lost or gained. It was only after Failson had spoken that other commentators pointed out that in these shows Barons had found his metier, with just the right combination of cleverness and common touch. The scandal soon blew over and was forgotten. The people's need for entertainment should not be underestimated.

Watching *Death of the Week, Month* or *Year* became a ritual in millions of homes. The stories of why people wanted to die were infinitely varied, as varied as life itself but more condensed. A few lone voices suggested that some postulants were lured or seduced into death by the hope of a moment's fame, but Frailson pointed out that this was a paternalistic argument, an assault on their personal autonomy. Anyone over the age of fourteen was fully capable of deciding for himself whether he wanted to live or die.

Another criticism occasionally heard was that most of the winners of the big prizes were white, male, young and handsome. It was they who were chosen by the viewers, who voted for them. But this was easily changed for the better: after all, it is not who votes that counts, but who counts the votes.

But after some years of uninterrupted success, a more serious criticism of Barons was heard: that he was beginning to age and lose his geniality. Indeed, on one occasion he seemed to lose his patience with a postulant, suggesting that he had no good reason for wanting to die and was a fool. The producer and editor of the episode in which this happened were, of course, sacked for incompetence for letting it be broadcast; but all the same, an article appeared in the *Times* under the title *Barons: the Mask Slips?*

Then people began to notice that Barons was losing weight. He had never been fat, of course; he had always been fit rather than athletic. Now he began to look gaunt, even emaciated. Occasionally he would grimace, as if he had just received an electric shock. Whereas before he had pranced around the studio or the set in the thanatoria with the enthusiasm of a puppy, he now remained as if glued to the chair in which he sat.

His stage of emaciation was succeeded by one of bloatedness. Is he on steroids, asked the celebrity columnists, always delighted at the misfortunes of others about whom they wrote: their drug addiction, divorces, accidents, ravages of age, troubles with the tax authorities. The answer in this case was yes, Barons was on steroids. This accounted for his increasingly erratic mood. He was also obviously on morphine, or something similar: you could see his pinpoint pupils. All of it could mean only one thing: cancer.

They were right. Of course, as soon as Barons had felt a decline from his accustomed rude health, which he attributed to his diet and his exercise, he sought the best medical attention available. Alas, the doctors, of whom he consulted many, were unanimous in their verdict. The cancer had gone to his spine and elsewhere, hence the deep gnawing pain that he suffered, slightly relieved only by ever-larger doses of drugs that ruined his mind. The prognosis was poor: decline, pain and suffering, and death.

But Barons had never been a man passively to accept the *force majeure* of fate. All his business career he had done what others, who thought themselves wiser than he, had told him was impossible to do, and he had proved them wrong, in the process building an immense fortune. He had been impatient of obstruction and had overcome it. He regarded his doctors as he had regarded the stick-in-the-mud bankers of yore who had stood in the way because of the supposed unviability of his schemes. Fools! They didn't know with whom they had to deal.

He began to research for himself, and set assistants on the research also when he was too sapped of energy to continue. His doctors seemed to be right, but there was a clinic in Mexico, in Yucatan, run by a renegade scientist, a former geophysicist, who had developed a curative formula (according to a plethora of testimonials), initially founded on a mixture of modern chemistry and ancient Olmec wisdom.

Barons flew to Mexico in his private jet. It was a long way from the Indian Ocean, and though his jet was of maximum luxuriousness, he arrived exhausted and in pain. His wife did not accompany him because he had long surrounded himself with pretty young women to prove his undiminished potency, and though she had not divorced him, they lived entirely separate lives. When his jet and its crew flew off, he was on his own in Yucatan.

His room in the clinic opened to the sea breeze and to the soothingly rhythmical sound of the waves reaching the shore just beyond was added the sound of wind-chimes in the semi-tropical trees, giving to the atmosphere a faintly Buddhist aura. The founder, owner and director of the Yucatan Mayan Wellness Clinic, Dr Fulvio González, had developed a guava vinegar and decoction of pine needles that caused regression of cancers, if combined with cranial massage and green tea enemas. Pain was the body's natural way of warning us that something was wrong, and therefore not to be suppressed; vomiting was the body's way of rejecting toxins. Therefore he stopped all the medications with which Barons had arrived.

Barons was in terrible pain, but too weak to protest. He was reduced to a skeleton. His teeth loosened. Sores appeared on his skin, which was no longer smooth. His room smelled of his own decay but fortunately he could not smell it. This was his only mercy.

Barons died in the early hours of a Thursday morning. He was buried within twenty-four hours in the municipal cemetery of San Marcos Xocatipula.

NOT A LEG TO STAND ON

AMOS WILSON was not a happy man. What had his parents – actually, his father – been thinking of when they, or he, gave him such a name? He had been mocked for it as a child and had never recovered from the mockery. The child, after all, is father to the man.

There was another serious reason for his unhappiness, however. Now aged forty, he had never known what every man desires, sexual fulfilment. For some reason which he could not fathom himself, there was no satisfaction for him in any sexual activity unless he imagined himself to be an amputee. He knew that this was, by the standards of others, strange, bizarre: but which of us can account for his desires, how and why they arise?

Fantasy is all very well, it is better than nothing at all, but it is no substitute for reality. By middle age, Amos had had enough of it and its pretences. Why should he be condemned to a second-rate life just because, through no fault of his own, he had developed a unusual desire that, if fulfilled, would harm no one else? Every man has a right to fulfilment.

He didn't tell anyone about his desire, of course. Everyone in the bank in which he worked thought he was a decent chap, perfectly ordinary except that he had never married: and even that these days was hardly abnormal. Men did not commit these days in case something better came along.

It was high time to declare himself, he thought: he did not want to die not having lived. His first step then, was to tell his doctor. After all, amputation was a medical procedure.

Dr Smith was a doctor of the old school. He was of the opinion that it was the duty of the patient to carry out his orders. For the most part, his orders did them good, but his manner was abrasive and he gave the impression of not suffering fools – ninety-five per cent of the population – gladly. It took courage to confide in him.

Amos plucked up that courage. As he came into Dr Smith's consulting room, he felt himself being inspected even before he sat down. Dr Smith peered at him over the top of his half-moon gold-rimmed spectacles, which gave him an air of unassuageable scepticism.

'What can I do for you?' he asked.

At least Amos was not an habitual complainer, or one of those patients who regarded a visit to the doctor as the highlight of his week. There was at least a fair chance, then, that he really had something wrong with him, one of an elite among Dr Smith's patients.

'I need help, doctor,' said Amos.

'What kind of help?'

'I have a problem.'

Dr Smith shifted slightly in his seat, a boatswain's chair. He was not a man for the elliptical approach to things.

'What kind of problem?' he said. 'Spit it out.'

'I've had it a long time,' said Amos, looking awkward or even guilty. 'All my life in fact, at least since I was grown up.'

Dr Smith had seven minutes for each patient, eight at most.

'What is it?' he asked. 'We haven't got all day.' And he looked at his watch, not to inform himself of the time, which he already knew from the clock on the wall opposite him whose second-hand emitted a faint clicking sound, but to indicate that he was busy.

Oddly enough, Dr Smith's brusqueness made it easier for Amos. It was now or never, and it gave him the courage of the desperate.

'I want my leg off,' he said.

'What?'

'I want my leg off.'

'Whatever for? What's wrong with your leg?'

'I've got one too many. I've always felt that, ever since I can remember. It's not mine, it's alien.'

Dr Smith removed his spectacles and placed them carefully on the top of his desk. He had never heard anything like it.

'What do you mean?' he asked. Two, after all, was the normal complement, not the object for a museum of pathology with Siamese twins in bottles of spirit.

'I feel I ought to have been born with one,' said Amos. 'The fact is that I can't have proper sex with two legs. I have to imagine all the time that I have only one.'

'So you want your leg off?' said Dr Smith weakly.

'Yes,' said Amos, 'so that I can have normal sex.'

'Normal sex? What do you mean by that?'

'Sex that satisfies me, in the same way that it satisfies everyone else. After all, it's my right. I don't see why everyone else should have it but I can't.'

Amos was warming to his theme now that he had broached it. He began to see that he had been oppressed all his life, persecuted in fact. He sensed that Dr Smith was on the side of the persecutors.

'I want an amputation.'

Dr Smith had recaptured his confidence, his certainty. You could tell this because he had picked up his spectacles and placed them back on the end of his nose.

'It's out of the question,' he said. 'No surgeon would agree to cut off a perfectly healthy leg.'

'Not even if I paid him?' asked Amos.

'Not even if you paid him. He'd never be allowed to practice again if anyone found out that he's carried out an amputation just for money.'

'He wouldn't be doing it just for money,' corrected Amos. 'He'd be doing it to help me.'

'Doctors are not here just to give patients what they want,

you know,' said Dr Smith. He too could warm to his subject. 'We have to do what is right for the patients, and cutting off perfectly sound limbs is not right. What if you came here and asked for both of your legs to be cut off?'

'That would be ridiculous and in any case, I haven't.'

'And what would you do afterwards, after your leg had been cut off? You'd be handicapped, a cripple.'

'Artificial legs are very good these days,' said Amos. 'There are people walking about with them that you wouldn't know had them. I'd take my leg off only when I wanted sex.'

'Who'd want sex with a one-legged man, especially when she knew that he had had the other leg cut off deliberately just so that he could get excited?'

Amos became coldly rational, unlike Dr Smith.

'It may surprise you to know that there are women around who want sex only with men with one leg. I don't see why they should be deprived of their satisfaction too.'

'Natural amputees,' said Dr Smith, 'that's different. They have their legs off for strictly medical reasons, not to gratify their, or anyone else's, perversions.'

Amos was horrified by the strength of Dr Smith's prejudice – and him an educated man!

'My body belongs to me,' said Amos, 'and it's my leg. I can do what I like with it. It's nobody else's business.'

'It is somebody else's business when you ask someone else to cut it off for you.'

Amos had never been much of a philosopher, but he suddenly discovered that he was one after all.

'Surgeons perform plenty of operations for non-medical reasons,' he said. 'Face-lifts for one.'

'That's to bring about improvement, not mutilation.'

'Who's to say what improvement is?' said Amos. 'Only the patient, it's up to him to decide. And I can tell you that my life would be much better with only one leg.'

Dr Smith was exasperated.

'Having your leg off is irreversible,' he said.

'So's having a facelift. So's having your appendix out.'

'That's to save your life.'

'A facelift isn't. And I know plenty of people who had their appendix out whose appendix was normal.'

'It does no harm. You don't need your appendix.'

'And I don't need my leg, on the contrary. It's in the way of my happiness. It prevents me from having a normal life.'

'Amputees don't have a normal life.'

'What are you saying? That amputees are not normal?'

'I'm going to bring this consultation to a close,' said Dr Smith. 'It's getting nowhere. You can't have your leg off and there's nothing further to say.'

Amos rose to go.

'We'll see about that,' he said, with steel in his voice.

On his way home, Amos replayed the consultation on his mind's video. From the purely dialectical point of view, he thought, and on the whole, he had had the better of it, but winning an argument is not the same as getting what you want. Besides, there were things that he should have said but didn't. And what, for example, if Dr Smith had used the argument that amputees imposed costs on others because they needed special arrangements? It was best to be prepared in advance in the coming struggle.

What was the answer? Yes, that was it: all the arrangements necessary for so-called voluntary amputees should have been made already, so another group of amputees should make no difference. Besides, arrangements were made to rescue mountaineers, and what benefits did mountaineers bring to society? Why should those who wanted only one leg be discriminated against?

Amos began to grow angry at the thought of it. People were so narrow-minded, censorious and intolerant: they judged you without knowing anything about you or making any effort to imagine what it would be like to be you. They just assumed that everyone was like themselves, or ought to have been so. They didn't want anyone to be different.

But what to do about it? Amos decided to try Dr Smith again, give him another chance: he might have thought better of what he had said and changed his attitude, though this was very unlikely.

Dr Smith had not changed his mind, on the contrary. He said that Amos should just forget the whole thing and carry on as best he could. He wanted to hear no more of it and his decision was final.

His obstinacy infuriated Amos, who was not usually quick to anger.

'If you don't help me, I'll make other arrangements,' he said.

'What do you mean by that?' asked Dr Smith.

'I'll amputate myself,' said Amos. 'There was a Russian doctor who took out his own appendix in a submarine when it was under the ice.'

'Don't be absurd. He was a trained man.'

'I can learn.'

In fact, he had already bought a couple of books on anatomy and orthopaedic surgery (the internal organs did not interest him). He thought that perhaps he should practice first on a dog or cat or two, but that was illegal and would cause great distress to their owners if discovered. There was enough misery in the world without adding to it.

He read about war, particularly in the Nineteenth Century, when soldiers regularly had their arms or legs blown off by cannonballs and other projectiles. Many of them survived even though they didn't have blood transfusions in those days, or antibiotics for that matter.

Amos' hopes that he might not have to resort to extreme measures were briefly raised when by chance he read in the newspaper of a surgeon who had been willing to amputate limbs for people like himself (so you see, Dr Smith, there were others like him); but his hopes were dashed when he read further that the surgeon had been disciplined and told that if he persisted – he had done it for money – he would be prohibited from further practice.

There was no prospect of official help, then: Amos would have to arrange things for himself. The best method, he decided, would be by train, you couldn't get a cleaner break than that.

It probably wouldn't even hurt, at least not at first, not if the stories from the battlefield were to be believed. Soldiers who had had their arms or legs blown off often didn't even realise it at first, not until they were removed from the scene. It was only when doctors and others started to fuss around them that they began to suffer, and these days it was easy to control pain. It was just a matter of taking drugs until the pain went away of its own accord.

But then a thought came into Amos' mind that he should seize the opportunity to do something for others, not just himself, indeed for his country and humanity as a whole. Until then, he realised, he had been thinking only of himself. But of course there were others suffering just like he. The public was lamentably ignorant, ill-informed, indifferent or hostile. Here was a golden opportunity to do something, the first time in his life that he had such a one. Amos began to think of himself as a leader, the leader of a movement, the Herzl of amputees.

How to begin his campaign? The obvious thing was to write an article for the *Clarion*, the famous newspaper that specialised in righting wrongs and fighting for the oppressed, giving voice to the voiceless. Once a week it allowed a completely unknown person to air his grievances (provided that, to be assuaged, they required radical reform). The article would also appear on the newspaper's website, which was read around the world.

Although he had never written anything before, passion caused Amos' pen to flow.

We are proud (he wrote) of our supposedly tolerant society. It is true that in some respects we are more tolerant than we were, but that it was not a difficult standard to raise, and there is still much to do. It's high time we broke the last taboo.

Amos was very pleased with that. It struck just the right note, for the newspaper was ever in search of last taboos to break. It gave them a sense of purpose.

Some people (he continued), of whom I am one, can only obtain sexual satisfaction if they have only one leg. It is not our fault we are like this, it is a fact of our nature over which we have no control.

We were born like it.

Amos then turned philosophical:

Everyone is agreed that a fulfilled sexual existence is a precondition of the good life, especially nowadays when we are surrounded by sexualised images. But we are denied this by ignorance and prejudice, principally but not only of the medical profession. We wish and do no harm to others, which – if we did it – would be the only grounds on which our desires could justifiably be denied. While everyone else receives public assistance to live full and satisfying lives, we alone do not because of the deep prejudice against us. We are the object of the most naked and blatant discrimination. We are the niggers of sex.

The phrase pleased him, though it was daring and he doubted that the *Clarion* would allow it. It wasn't meant in a racist way, of course, precisely the opposite: but the use of the word in any context was taboo. When the article was published, however, the word was left in (after a long discussion by the editors). It was merely changed to 'We feel like the niggers of sex.'

The article had an immense impact. There were thousands of comments on it, ranging from expressions of support (at last someone has had the courage to come forward) to those who thought that all the author's limbs and other parts ought to be cut off without anaesthetic. Amos found himself besieged by requests for interviews. He was a celebrity overnight.

The interviews were all the same.

'When did you first realise that you wanted to be an amputee?'

'Do you think it is normal to want to be an amputee?'

'How many people are there like you, do you think?'

'Should there be amputation on demand?'

Repetition allowed Amos to refine his answers. Before long he felt like a tape-recorder being played over and over again. Amputation, he said, should always be performed by a qualified surgeon because, if it were not, people would die, either by suicide or by performing it themselves. The latter would either resort to railway lines or to unqualified persons.

'Do you know of cases where people have actually done that?' he was always asked. 'And if so, how many?'

With a patience that by no means corresponded to his inner state of mind, he would reply that it was impossible to say, because the subject was so taboo that no proper research had ever been done. Auto-amputations would be recorded as accidents rather than what they really were.

It was obvious to Amos, however, that after the initial flurry, the interest would die down: public attention was like a butterfly that flitted from flower to flower and seldom returned. Something more was needed.

At least twenty people with the same interests as Amos, so to speak, contacted him and they decided to form an association to be called the UBC, Unipeds By Choice. This would distinguish them from amputees that had been involved in an accident or had had gangrene from diabetes and smoking. One of the twenty, fortunately, was an expert in the design of websites, and before long there was a lot of what he called traffic. Most visitors to the site were merely curious or prurient, wanting a frisson of disgust or disdain, an opportunity to exercise their sarcasm. Everyone, after all, needs to feel superior to someone, and most people who visited the site could say to themselves or others, 'At least I'm not like that!'

But increasingly there were enquiries from the seriously interested. Writing that they were desperate, they asked where they might have their legs off. The site began to act as in an information exchange. The names of surgeons and clinics in foreign countries where, for a fee, they were prepared to perform amputations were listed, followed by a lively debate on the injustice of this. Why should only the well-to-do have the right to amputations? Moreover, there were warnings about some of the foreign surgeons and clinics. They took your money all right, but they could be dangerous. Stories began to appear of death by haemorrhage or infection, and even of arrests and imprisonment in dark and terrible gaols, and the bribes necessary to get out. Going abroad, then, was not the panacea it had for a time been presented as having been.

It was obvious to Amos and those who he now called his colleagues that the only way forward was a proper amputation service in the country itself. It had to be free of commercial interest, of course, for nothing would have been easier for the anti-amputee lobby to impute corruption wherever money changed hands. The service, then, would have to be staffed by believers in the cause, those who amputated by conviction. But competent surgeons would not be enough, it was just as important that amputations should be performed responsibly, not just on a passing whim. It was necessary, therefore, that psychiatrists and psychologists be involved, to ensure that those who wanted a leg (or more rarely an arm) off were stable, of normal personality and fully aware of the implications of the operation.

The first problem was to find a willing surgeon. This was despite the fact that there had been a burgeoning number of people – seven eights of them men – who expressed an interest in having a limb off. There was a brief spark of hope when a surgeon in a small town in Wales declared himself willing, but the hope was extinguished when he was forced to retract and sent on a course on medical ethics.

However, his highly-publicised martyrdom proved a blessing in disguise, because it gave the group the opportunity to publicise the sad plight of people like themselves. The group started a petition in the surgeon's favour which was signed by more than a hundred thousand people, and although this produced no tangible effect in official circles, it began to change the attitude of the general public, or that part of it that spoke of abstract matters such as rights. When the subject now came up at dinner parties (which was surprisingly often), people began to say, 'Why not after all?'

But though Amos was pleased and even proud of the progress that had been achieved, he was impatient because the clock was still ticking for him and he no longer thought of himself as young. Eventual triumph in the struggle for freedom was all very well, and would be a good thing, but it could hardly satisfy him personally. His closest associate in the movement, whom he had met only via the computer screen, suggested that what was needed was a publicity coup.

What should it be?

Amos and his colleague devised a plan. Amos would be the first, but not the last, to perform an auto-amputation on a railway line. Of course, it would have to be perfectly planned, not an impulsive act. He would do it in the presence of his colleague (who was called Sam). The first time they met in person would be at the track, but before that they made sure that they had learnt how to staunch bleeding and apply pressure bandages. Amos reconnoitred the local railway lines for a place suitable for the operation. It had to be isolated enough to be away from prying eyes, yet easy of access for the ambulance that Sam would call immediately on the approach of the amputating train. Sam would make himself scarce, of course, as soon as the ambulance appeared and would use a temporary telephone number to make his call, to avoid any possible imputation of crime. And they would also have to find a trustworthy person to take a proper film of the event, preferably of professional quality, to post on the internet. They found such a person in William, a student of media studies at the local university, who had also expressed an interest in having his leg off. The film would alert the world to the lengths to which desperate people would go in the present oppressive circumstances; it would shock and inform at the same time.

They had no doubt of its success, but a nine-day wonder was not enough. They had to keep the pressure up: a corpse of a moribund society needed repeated shocks to bring it back to life – if it had ever really been alive. They planned what they called 'future events.'

The day of the first action arrived. The place they had chosen was a line very near a road but hidden by a little covert of birch. To Amos' regret, it would have to be a below-knee amputation because it was too awkward to manoeuvre one of his thighs on the rail and it was advisable to lie comfortably while waiting for the train.

They had, of course, researched the train timetable thoroughly. They had selected the train that was to perform the surgery, an express passenger that would not be able to slow to less than eighty miles an hour between the moment when the driver first saw Amos and the time it reached him.

William filmed Amos for a few minutes lying in the ground with one leg extended over the rail before the arrival of the train. Amos looked cheerful and gave the thumbs-up sign, though he was of course feeling a little nervous. Would he be able to go through with it, or would he change his mind at the last moment? He was determined, but one never knew.

The train approached. Amos could feel the vibrations in his leg when it was a long way off. Sam called the ambulance so that it would arrive very shortly after the operation had been performed, and he gave the controller Amos' precise GPS position as well as providing a detailed verbal description of where he was lying. Sam put his hand on Amos' shoulder to steady him. He, too, wanted the action to be a success.

It all went precisely as planned. The train was on time and was not able to stop before removing Amos' leg. William filmed it, carefully avowing not to include any picture of Sam applying the bandage afterwards. Intolerance imposed the need for anonymity.

The event would have made only the local newspaper, and perhaps not even that, had it not been filmed and posted afterwards. The doctors at the local hospital were astounded at what Amos had done (a hospital nearby had been another criterion of choice of location) because they had never had a case like his before, such was their inexperience and lack of imagination. But Amos' wider fame did not spread until the film of the operation was posted.

At first Amos felt no pain: his exultation conquered his nerve endings. Then the pain began, but they treated him with drugs that detached him from reality and left him as if floating on a cloud. But when he woke up from the hospital operation to 'tidy up' his stump, as the surgeon called it, he was delighted to find that his amputation had been extended to above the knee, which of course was much more what he had desired. It was held in much more esteem than the below-knee type.

It was only after the first posting of the video that Amos' fame really spread. It was not fame, however, that Amos, Sam and William had sought, but acceptance and reform. What business was it of anyone, after all, to pass judgment on them? Was a human being constituted solely by the number of his limbs? Did anyone refuse to admire or obey Admiral Nelson because he had only one arm? It would have been different, of course, if they had been demanding amputations for others, but they were not.

The second part of the plan was now put into effect. A youth or young man of seventeen volunteered to have the same operation performed on him by a passing train. Unfortunately, it was not such a success and the young man bled to death. For some reason the bandages were not applied properly and the arrival of the ambulance was delayed, and it was on the delay that the national press focussed. 'This case illustrates the cruel and criminal folly,' said the editorial about it in the *Clarion*, 'of budgetary cuts that overstrain the ambulance services to breaking point. The fiscal fetish kills.'

But the death of the young man only accelerated the next stage of the plan, which Amos and Sam called 'a mass amputation.'

The arrangement needed extra care because the railway authorities were beginning to display extra vigilance, hurriedly installing cameras up and down lines: but of course this was futile because it was impossible to cover more than a small proportion of the network, some of the cameras didn't work anyway, and with typical bureaucratic incompetence they were often placed where they would never have dreamt of carrying out an action anyway, where no one in his right mind would consider amputating his leg. The plan needed a large number of volunteers to ensure its success.

The great day came, the day that was to change the nation. Eight people, only one of them a woman, lay down their limbs, or put their limbs on the line (literally), for the cause of social progress and sexual fulfilment. (Only one of the limbs was an arm.) This time it was a great success, with only one death, and that solely because the local hospital had run out of ambulances. The event was a triumph of determination and organisation, conducted in the utmost secrecy, having completely evaded the authorities beforehand. They had used a clever diversionary tactic, sending a group of supporters to a line not far distant from where the real event was to take place. By advertising their presence, they had drawn the attention of the police and other authorities away from that place. A few of the diverters had been arrested for trespassing on railway property, but this slight martyrdom was a small price to pay for the success of the liberating *coup de théâtre*.

This time, the event was reported nationally and *ad nauseam*. Members of Parliament appeared on television to demand that henceforth surgeons be obliged to cut off the limbs of those who wanted them amputated. This, they said, was the only way to stop the carnage. Neuroscientists appeared on the television to demonstrate what parts of the amputees' brains lit up or failed to light up on scans before and after their limbs were cut off.

Amos, whose injury had by this time healed sufficiently and had learned to manipulate his crutches before he was fitted with the latest in artificial legs, appeared many times on television, usually described as the victim of the current dispensation. But though he agreed with the Members of Parliament as far as they went, he said that what was needed was more than a reform of the law. The fundamental problem, he said, was what he called *quadrilimbism*, the assumption that human beings have four limbs and that any deviation from the hegemonic pattern was bizarre, abnormal or pathological. For example, the illustrations of all children's books, apart from *Treasure Island*, showed characters only with four limbs, that is to say two arms and two legs. This indoctrinated children with the idea that people with one or more limbs missing were abnormal in some way. He also suggested that from now on the word amputee should no longer be used, as it had derogatory connotations of disability or even inability. He suggested that from now on amputees be known as the differently-limbed. As for the inclusion of apotemnophilia and acrotomophilia in textbooks of psychopathology, he suggested that the pages be torn out. The mediaeval witch–hunt of the quadrilimbists against the differently-limbed had to stop.

The government quickly passed a bill, without opposition, obliging surgeons to amputate the limbs of adults above the age of fourteen who wanted them amputated (the parents of the fourteen year olds were specifically not to be informed) and from now on it was inscribed in the code of medical ethics that no doctor could refuse to assist such a person in finding a surgeon to perform the operation, henceforth to be known as limb correction. Once the bill was passed, thousands of people came forward for limb correction (mainly legs), and soon there were so many people waiting for the operation that it became a national disgrace. The solution was to train nurses to cut off legs, though arms, being more difficult to sever, remained the province of full surgeons.

There was still much to do to remove prejudice, but Amos was pleased to see that publishers were now printing children's books with pictures of Mummy and Daddy (or just Mummy) with fewer than four limbs, and some with no limbs at all. In some primary schools, children were being taught a course against quadrilimbism, and he hoped that these courses would become compulsory everywhere.

After a prolonged period of sick leave because of anxiety, two of the three train drivers whose trains had performed the initial operations killed themselves.

CPSIA information can be obtained
at www.ICGtesting.com
Printed in the USA
LVHW101133280223
740522LV00005B/246